"You wouldn't unders

Parker stepped closer still. "How do you know?"

"Because you have all of this." Kayleigh gestured around them angrily, fresh tears stinging her eyes. "You have no idea what I'm feeling right now, and I hope you never do."

He stepped closer, his voice low and his expression sincere. "I would never have invited you if I'd realized how it would impact you."

"It isn't your fault." She sniffled. "I can't remember the last time I cried about losing my mom."

Parker lifted his hands and cradled her jaw and he lowered his head.

His lips met hers in a kiss that was tender and sweet. Yet her body burned for him.

She did want this. His firm, sensual lips pressed to hers. His strong hands gently cradling her face. His hard body braced against hers.

She gasped when he lifted her onto the table, without breaking their kiss.

The ridge beneath his zipper pressed against the growing heat between her thighs.

Making her want things with Parker Abbott.

Things that she *shouldn't* want...

* * *

Engaging the Enemy is part of the Bourbon Brothers series from Reese Ryan.

Dear Reader,

Welcome back to my Bourbon Brothers series set in the tiny fictional town of Magnolia Lake, Tennessee. This series follows the drama-filled romantic adventures of the five Abbott siblings—four of whom help run the world-renowned King's Finest Distillery.

In *Engaging the Enemy*, Parker Abbott will do whatever it takes to acquire the run-down old building owned by his childhood best friend, jewelry artist Kayleigh Jemison. He'll even pose as Kayleigh's fiancé during the island wedding of her ex's sister. But their fake relationship exposes very real feelings neither of them is prepared to face.

Thank you for joining me for the passion, secrets and drama of my Bourbon Brothers series. If you have a question or comment about this series or others, visit reeseryan.com/desirereaders to drop me a line. While you're there, be sure to join my VIP Readers newsletter list for series news, reader giveaways and more.

Until our next adventure,

Reese

REESE RYAN

———

ENGAGING THE ENEMY

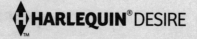

Recycling programs
for this product may
not exist in your area.

ISBN-13: 978-1-335-60359-3

Engaging the Enemy

Printed in U.S.A.

www.Harlequin.com

Reese Ryan writes sexy, deeply emotional romances full of family drama, surprising secrets and unexpected twists.

Born and raised in the Midwest, Reese has deep Tennessee roots. Every summer, she endured long, hot car trips to family reunions in Memphis via a tiny clown car loaded with cousins.

Connect with Reese at ReeseRyanWrites on Instagram, Twitter and Facebook, or at reeseryan.com/desirereaders.

Books by Reese Ryan

Harlequin Desire

The Bourbon Brothers

Savannah's Secret
The Billionaire's Legacy
Engaging the Enemy

Texas Cattleman's Club: Bachelor Auction

His Until Midnight

Harlequin Kimani Romance

Playing with Desire
Playing with Temptation
Playing with Seduction

To all of the fantastic, supportive readers in my Reese Ryan VIP Readers Lounge on Facebook. You've made this journey truly remarkable. As long as you keep reading my stories, I'll keep writing them.

To Johnathan Royal and Stephanie Perkins, thank you for being not only loyal readers, but such vocal advocates. You enthusiastically champion my work and introduce new readers to it. I am tremendously grateful to both of you!

To Charles Griemsman, you're a patient, insightful editor. You challenge me in ways that deepen my characters, strengthen my story and make me a better storyteller. I'm glad we're a team.

One

Parker Abbott pulled into the parking lot of the two-story building that had definitely seen better days.

Better decades even.

He parked, turned off the engine and groaned.

Kayleigh.

His high school nemesis and the one person in town who was most likely to head up the Parker Abbott *not-a-fan* club.

Usually he enjoyed negotiating deals for their family-owned distillery. But the thought of negotiating anything with Kayleigh made a knot form in his gut.

Perhaps because, deep down, he still saw her as the girl with curly pigtails and thick glasses who had once been his closest friend. Until a falling-out had made them bitter adversaries.

Parker heaved a sigh, pushed open the car door and climbed to his feet.

Waiting five more minutes, or even five more days, wouldn't make the task ahead any easier.

Parker straightened his tie and grabbed his attaché from the back seat of the car. He wasn't that preteen boy with a killer crush on Kayleigh Jemison anymore. He was a goddamned professional, and he was going to act like it, even if it killed him.

As Parker approached the shop, he caught sight of Kayleigh's shock of coppery-red curls through the window. She was gorgeous, as always, with her honey-brown skin and expressive coffee-brown eyes.

Kayleigh was laughing with a customer, but as she waved goodbye to the woman, she caught a glimpse of him standing outside, gawking at her.

Her deep scowl and hard stare confirmed exactly what he'd expected. Kayleigh Jemison was going to give him hell.

He reached into his pocket, flipped the top on a tube of antacids and popped two into his mouth.

Kayleigh Jemison folded her arms as she stared through the window of her small handmade-jewelry-and-consignment shop.

What the hell was he doing there? It wasn't Christmas and his mother's and sister's birthdays weren't imminent. And the uptight, Wall-Street-wannabe certainly wasn't the kind of man who'd wear her hand-tooled jewelry. So why was he here? And why on earth was he staring at her like she was a museum exhibit?

Kayleigh involuntarily dragged her fingers through her wild red curls, trying to create some semblance of order.

It was a slow weekday, so she'd been in the back, stamping and hammering metal pieces to be shipped to customers across the country. She wore a faded old T-shirt and a tattered pair of jeans stained with leather dye. A black bandanna pulled her hair back.

In short, she looked a hot damn mess.

Of all the days for him to show up at her shop… Kayleigh sighed, giving up any hope of redeeming her look.

What did it matter anyway?

As far as Parker was concerned, she was beneath the mighty Abbotts. They were the family with the keys to the kingdom in their growing small town of Magnolia Lake, Tennessee, a gem situated in the foothills of the picturesque Smoky Mountains.

The Abbotts, owners of King's Finest Distillery, the largest local employer, were well-known and beloved by everyone in town.

Except her.

The little bell over the entrance tinkled when Parker yanked open the door, holding it for the customer who was leaving. The woman was juggling her purse, her bags and an unruly toddler.

So he does have manners. He just uses them selectively.

"Parker Abbott, what brings you into my shop today?" Kayleigh stood straight as a rod and tried to relax her involuntary scowl.

She'd returned to Magnolia Lake to start a business

after going to college in Nashville and then living in Atlanta. Waging an outright war with the Abbotts would be detrimental to her interests. Besides, despite her disdain for Parker and his father, his mother and sister were nice enough. They'd been longtime customers and had referred lots of other clients. They'd even invited her to sell a few of her higher-end pieces on consignment at the distillery gift shop.

It was a lucrative partnership. So despite her utter disdain for the man who'd once been her closest friend, but betrayed her without the slightest hint of an apology, she would play nice.

For now.

"I wondered if you planned on coming in or if you were auditioning to be a living statue."

Okay, maybe not exactly nice, but close enough.

He glared at her with his typical Parker Abbott glare, but then he did something beyond strange.

He actually *smiled.*

Or at least he was attempting to smile. He looked like Jack Nicholson as the Joker.

She kept that observation to herself, but she couldn't help the smirk that spread across her face.

"Good afternoon, Kayleigh," Parker said in a tone that was unnaturally cheerful for him. "I was hoping I could have a few minutes of your time, if you're not too busy."

Kayleigh scanned the empty store, but bit back a flippant response. "Sure. What can I do for you, Abbott?"

Parker relaxed and his smile looked a little more natural. "Actually, I'd like to do something for you."

"Is that right?" Kayleigh folded her arms, one eyebrow raised. "Now, what would that be?"

Parker indicated the two chaises placed back-to-back in the center of the store. "Would it be all right if we sat?"

Kayleigh shrugged. "Sure."

After Parker took a seat on one of the chaises, she sat at the opposite end and turned toward him, glancing at the leather cuff timepiece on her wrist. "You were saying?"

Parker was one of the most impatient men she knew. Why, for God's sake, wasn't he getting to the point? She had orders to complete and ship.

"I'd like to buy your store."

"What?"

Surely she'd misheard him. Why on earth would Parker want to do that? The man had no use for her jewelry; he only wore a watch. In fact he collected high-end timepieces purchased at seizure auctions and estate sales. But that was the extent of his jewelry collection, as far as she could tell.

Kayleigh schooled her features, determined not to show her surprise. "I'm sorry, did you say you want to purchase my store?"

Parker straightened his tie and made another attempt at a smile. This one was better. "Not the store, per se. What we're after is the building. You'd be free to re-establish the store wherever you'd like."

Kayleigh almost laughed. She pointed to the worn floorboards beneath her. "You want *this* building?"

She loved this place, but the old girl was falling

apart at the seams. She'd bought it five years ago, expecting it to be a long-term fixer-upper. But the building had required expensive repairs to the foundation, new plumbing and electrical rewiring. All of which had cost a bundle but had done little to improve the aesthetics.

The ancient roof had been patched more times than she cared to admit, and the HVAC system for the store was just about on its last legs. The nicest part of the building was the apartment she rented out upstairs. Her apartment, also upstairs, had plenty of shabby but very little chic.

"Why would you want to buy my building? The distillery is ten miles from here. And if you want a building in town, why not one built in that new multipurpose shopping center your brother is building up the road?"

There was a tick in Parker's jaw and his mask slipped. He seemed to be making a real effort to hide his annoyance, but it flickered in his dark eyes.

"We have plans for it."

It was evident that Parker didn't want to share those plans. At least not with her.

"Thank you for the offer, but my building isn't for sale," Kayleigh said politely, rising to her feet.

"You haven't even heard my offer." Parker stood, too.

"It doesn't matter what you're offering because the building isn't for sale." She folded her arms again.

"Despite its current condition, I'll give you the tax-assessed value of the building."

Though she knew the information was public, it made

her skin crawl to think that Parker had gone through her records. She scowled. "Thanks, but no thanks."

She walked behind the counter, hoping he'd get the hint.

"Kayleigh, you're being unreasonable. I'm making you a generous offer." When she didn't reply, he waved his large hand around the room. "My God, look at this place. No one in their right mind is going to give you full value for this building in the condition it's in now."

"I plan to fix the place up. Flip it, eventually."

"We both know that's not something you can afford. If you could, you surely would've replaced that old, leaky roof by now."

Kayleigh's face stung. It was one thing for her to disparage her old, run-down building; it was another thing altogether for the high-and-mighty Lord Parker Abbott to do it.

"You don't know anything about me or what I can afford," she seethed, her pulse racing.

"Then why haven't you—"

"I'll replace the damn roof when I'm good and ready."

Parker sighed, clearly exasperated that she hadn't fallen to her knees and kissed his expensive Italian loafers, thanking him for his "generous" offer.

"It's your first property and it's where you started your business. You're sentimental about the place. I get it. I'll offer you five percent above tax value."

"No." Kayleigh peered at him.

"Ten percent above."

"No." Her heart jackhammered in her chest. Partly because she was indignant that Parker Abbott thought he could just walk in off the street and steal her building right from under her. As if she was an inconsequential bug he could squash under his heel and then keep it moving. Partly because she realized she was acting contrary to her own best interest.

Parker was right. No one else would want this building in its current condition, and they certainly wouldn't give her the tax-assessed value for it.

"Dammit, Kayleigh, we're being more than generous here. You're just being obstinate for the sake of it. Forget for a moment that it's me making the offer and just think about it. You can move to that new shopping center that's going to get all that tourist traffic. It's a win-win for both of us."

"Is there a better way for me to say this? Hmm… Let me see… Hell to the no, Parker. My building isn't for sale."

Parker sighed heavily, as if the words he was conjuring were causing him physical pain. "All right, Kayleigh. What if we pay fifty percent more than the assessed value?"

Kayleigh's ears perked up. If cheap-ass Parker Abbott was offering to overpay for her building, he wanted the place desperately. Which meant she was the one with the leverage. This was the opportunity she'd been waiting for. A chance to reclaim some of what Duke Abbott had stolen from her family.

While she and her older sister, Evelisse, were away at college and her father was deathly ill, Duke had paid her mother a mere pittance for the land she'd inherited from Kayleigh's maternal grandfather. He'd taken advantage of her mother at her lowest point and robbed them of land that had been handed down in their family for generations.

Kayleigh stood taller, her chin tipped up as she met his intense gaze. "It would be nice to move my shop to the new mixed-use center, but as I'm sure you already know, leasing space there won't be cheap. And there's something else you haven't considered…"

"And what might that be?" Parker, the unofficial president of the Hard-core Perfectionists' Club, looked indignant at her insinuation that he'd overlooked something.

"This building doesn't just house my business. It's also my home. Then there's the rental income from the other apartment. While your offer seems generous on the surface…all things considered…it's a hard pass."

"That's why I'm offering you way more than this… *place*…is worth."

"But not enough if you expect me to move my shop, studio and apartment while also recouping lost rental income."

"No one's lived there since Savannah moved out three years ago," Parker said, referring to his sister-in-law and Kayleigh's closest friend.

"I make even more off it as an Airbnb," she said casually.

"Okay, fine. What figure would you consider adequate compensation?" Parker shoved his hands in his pockets and widened his stance.

Kayleigh's gaze was automatically drawn to the panel over his zipper and the outline of his…

Nope. Uh-uh. Hell no.

"Give me twice the tax-assessed value and I'll gladly hand the building over to you today. Lock, stock and barrel."

Parker looked like a volcano about to erupt. "Are you insane? Seriously, Kayleigh, you should be paying me to take this friggin' money pit off your hands. Like, right now, before the whole damn building falls down around us." He gestured wildly.

Before she could tell him exactly where he could shove his last offer, her phone rang. She blew out a hard breath and whipped her phone out of her pocket.

Kira Brennan.

Kayleigh hadn't seen or heard that name in more than seven years. She hadn't expected to ever again. So why was Kira Brennan calling her now?

Two

Kayleigh's back stiffened and her heart beat in double time as she stared at the number on her phone.

Kira was her ex-boyfriend's younger sister. And during the three years she'd dated Aidan Brennan, she'd been closer to Kira than she was to her own sister. But they hadn't spoken in years. What could she possibly want?

Kayleigh considered not answering the phone. Maybe it was best if she just let it go to voice mail. Then she could listen to the message and answer later, preferably by text.

The last time they'd spoken, Kira had been bitter and resentful. Kayleigh and Aidan had been together three years, and he'd started to hint at the possibility of marriage. But Kayleigh couldn't imagine herself as a member of the Brennan family.

Neither could their matriarch, Colleen Brennan.

Aidan's mother had told her, in no uncertain terms, that she'd merely tolerated their relationship as a phase Aidan needed to get out of his system. But she would never welcome Kayleigh into the Brennan family.

Mrs. Brennan had told Kayleigh that if she really loved Aidan, she'd do what was best for everyone and end the relationship, before things got any more serious between them.

Kayleigh had walked away. Not because his mother had asked her to, but because everything the woman said was true.

Except for Kira and Aidan, who both loved her, everyone else in the Brennan clan had seemed irritated and uptight every time she had shown up at another of their family functions. More important, as much as she'd loved Aidan, she just hadn't fit into his world.

She hadn't turned down his offer because she was intimidated by his mother; she'd done it because she'd genuinely believed it was in both their best interests.

She'd explained her position to Aidan, but chosen not to disclose her talk with his mother. He'd been crushed by her decision to walk away, and so had his sister.

So why was Kira calling her now?

"Kayleigh? Is everything all right?" Parker's voice was laced with what almost sounded like genuine concern.

"Absolutely." The last thing she wanted to do was reveal a chink in her armor to a shark like Parker Abbott. "And if you're not willing to meet my number, the answer is still no."

"But, Kayleigh—"

Her phone rang again. *Kira.*

Panic gripped her chest. If Kira was so determined to reach her after all this time, there had to be a reason. Her brother had moved on. He'd found someone else. Someone more to Mrs. Brennan's liking. They'd gotten married and had their first child all in the space of one year.

But maybe Kira was calling because something had happened to her brother.

"I need to take this call." Kayleigh held up a finger. She turned her back to Parker and walked a few paces away.

"Hello?"

"Kayleigh! Thank God you answered! I hate leaving voice mails. I never know what to say, especially on an occasion like this."

Kira was still an energetic chatterbox. And even after all this time, she knew she didn't need to identify herself. That Kayleigh would just know who she was.

"It's good to hear from you, Kira." Kayleigh smiled. "Especially after the way we left things—"

"I know… I was a stupid kid. I didn't mean any of those awful things I said, but I was so hurt and angry. I know that's no excuse, but—"

"It's okay, Kira. I realize how hard it must've been for you to understand why I did what I did."

"I do understand. Mother told me about the conversation she had with you after Aidan asked her for our grandmother's wedding ring. I only wish you'd told us instead of just walking away."

"Does he know?" Kayleigh cast a glance over her shoulder at Parker, who was pacing the floor.

He tapped on the face of his black Hermès watch with a double leather strap.

Kayleigh considered holding up a different finger, but held up her index finger instead and dipped behind the curtain to her studio space in the back.

"No. She wouldn't have told me, but I figured it out from something she said when she was a little…shall we say tipsy? The next morning she begged me not to tell Aidan, and I caved. Mostly because I know how much it would hurt him. And about Aidan—"

"I don't want to talk about Aidan." Kayleigh ran her fingers through her hair, probably making it look like even more of a crow's nest than it already did. "What's past is past."

"No problem. That isn't why I called anyway."

"So why did you call? Not that I'm not glad to hear from you."

"First I want to apologize for my behavior and for what my mother did."

"Apology accepted." Even if Kira was no longer in her life, it felt better knowing that the air between them had been cleared. "And what's the other reason?"

"To tell you that… I'm getting married!" Kira finished her sentence with a squeal. "Can you believe it?"

"Oh honey, that's wonderful news. I'm so happy for you."

"That's not even the best part…" Kira took a dramatic pause. "I want you to be in my wedding!"

"Me? Why?"

"Because my fiancé has a ton of brothers, and I want my bridesmaids to be people who have been truly important in my life. Not just some random, distant cousin filling up a spot. Our relationship meant so much to me. I want you to be there to share my day."

Kayleigh hesitated for a moment. "Are you sure this isn't just about pissing your mother off?"

"Well, there's that, too." Kira laughed. "But seriously, you mean a lot to me, Kayleigh."

"And Aidan and his wife won't be upset?"

"I guarantee you that Aidan's wife won't raise any objections." The humor was gone from her voice. "And neither will my brother. In fact I'm sure he'll be glad to see you again."

"I don't know, Kira. When's the wedding?"

"In two and a half months. And get this…my fiancé's family owns a private island in the Caribbean. That's where we're getting married. And we're flying everyone out for the entire week, all-expenses paid."

An all-expenses-paid vacation on an island in the Caribbean for an entire week? That was something to consider.

"Kira, I'm honored that you'd ask me to be part of your wedding—"

"Then you'll do it? Awesome! Just text me the name of your plus-one and all the information my wedding coordinator will need to book your flights. You're the best, Kayleigh. Bye!"

Kira had ended the call before Kayleigh could tell her

she'd *think* about it and that she most certainly didn't have a plus-one.

She scrubbed a hand across her forehead and sighed. The truth was that, as reluctant as she was to do this, she'd always had a soft spot for Kira. So they both knew she'd eventually cave.

Besides, maybe by the time the wedding rolled around, she would actually have a plus-one prospect.

She shoved her phone into her back pocket and returned to the front of the store, where Parker looked fit to be tied.

Parker stared at Kayleigh. He'd bet she took that call in the middle of their negotiations just to tick him off.

If that was her aim, she'd succeeded.

He was a busy man. He'd scheduled exactly thirty-five minutes for this meeting. It was already going on forty-five minutes and they hadn't agreed on anything.

Kayleigh was being stubborn. No, downright ornery. Was she really going to allow her disdain for him to prevent her from accepting his exceedingly generous offer?

"So, where were we?" Kayleigh seemed distracted and her hair looked even wilder than it had when she'd disappeared behind the curtain. As if she'd just tumbled out of bed and she hadn't been alone.

He swallowed hard, fighting off the image of Kayleigh in bed that immediately filled his brain.

Focus, Parker. Focus.

"I'd offered you fifty percent more than the assessed value."

She froze for a moment, cocking her head before

a smirk curled one corner of her mouth. "I remember now. You asked what figure would make me happy, and I said—"

"I know what you said, Kayleigh, and it's unacceptable."

"Then buy someone else's building instead." She stared at him defiantly.

The number-one rule of negotiating was be prepared to walk away. Every salesperson understood that. But his family hadn't given him that option. This building had once belonged to his mother's family. They'd run a tiny café here, and now his father wanted to help his mother reclaim a portion of her family's history by creating a flagship restaurant here, branded with the King's Finest name.

It was going to be a surprise. His mother didn't know, but his father had already purchased the two other buildings on the block and made the sellers sign confidentiality agreements. But without Kayleigh's building—the cornerstone of the entire project—it simply wouldn't work.

Closing this deal was the leverage he needed to make his father realize that naming his older brother, Blake, as his successor at King's Finest, simply because he'd had the good fortune to be born first, would be a grave mistake.

Blake was a good person, a great brother and an excellent operations manager. But neither Blake nor their brother Max possessed the killer instinct the CEO position called for. His sister, Zora, did have that killer instinct. More so than he, perhaps. But what she lacked was the ability to control her emotions. With Zora, everything was personal. She was much like Kayleigh in that way.

He had to have this building, but Kayleigh didn't know that. So maybe if he showed her that he was willing to walk away, she'd come to her senses.

Parker stooped to pick up his attaché. "Sorry we couldn't come to an agreement. Maybe it would be better if we went with new construction in that shopping center. I'm sure my brother will give us a good deal."

Parker crossed the room under Kayleigh's cold stare, waiting for her to stop him.

She didn't.

He turned the doorknob and stepped one foot onto the sidewalk, the bell jingling above him.

Still nothing.

"You really don't have anything else to say?" Parker turned back to her.

"Don't let the doorknob hit you where the good Lord split you." She grinned, her eyes shimmering with amusement.

Parker blew out an exasperated breath and stepped back inside. "Look, there has to be *something* we can do to sweeten the deal for you. I can do the one-point-five and throw in renovation of your new space so that it meets your specific needs. Or maybe an all-expenses paid vacation."

"What did you say?" She narrowed her gaze at him.

He now had Kayleigh's rapt attention.

"I said we can renovate your space so it fits your needs."

"Or…"

"Or throw in an all-expenses paid vacation." Something in Kayleigh's expression unnerved him. The wheels were definitely turning in her head.

"That." She shook a finger in his direction, her gaze not meeting his, as if she was still working everything out. "I want the all-expenses paid vacation, but you won't have to pay for it."

Parker scratched the back of his neck. Kayleigh Jemison had confounded him for years. He didn't think it was possible, but today she was more confusing than usual. "That doesn't make any sense. The whole point of the offer is to—"

"I know how negotiations work, Abbott," she said dismissively. "Just listen and don't panic while I tell you the rest."

Now Parker was really alarmed. He set his attaché on the floor again and shoved his hands in his pockets. "I'm listening."

"You pay me twice the property's assessed value. That will allow me to lease a new shop and buy a nice condo in the same complex."

Parker had no desire to overpay for Kayleigh's crumbling building, but his father had insisted that he do whatever it took to acquire the property. It was to be his anniversary gift to Parker's mother, and a sound investment for their business.

"I'll consider it," he said gruffly.

"But there's one more thing I need."

"In addition to us overpaying for the property?"

She didn't acknowledge the comment. "As a condition of our deal, you'll need to accompany me on a one-week, all-expenses paid trip to the Caribbean."

He stared at her for a moment, waiting for the punch line.

"But you despise me." When she didn't disagree, Parker leaned against a display case, his arms folded across his chest as he studied her. "Why would you want me, of all people, to accompany you?"

He wasn't always the best at reading people, but there was definitely something that Kayleigh was having a hard time getting out.

"You have to pretend to be my fiancé." She cringed as she said the words.

"What?" Parker pressed a hand to his forehead, stunned by her request. "You're not serious."

"You need this building for whatever your next big venture is, and I need a fake fiancé for a week. It's not as if I'm asking you to trade murders, Abbott. This isn't *Strangers on a Train*. Do you want this building or not?"

"There are escorts for this sort of thing, or have you not seen *The Wedding Date*?" he retorted. She wasn't the only one who could throw around a film reference to make a point.

"You're no Dermot Mulroney," she mumbled under her breath. "This isn't some romantic fantasy, and I have zero interest in sleeping with you. So if that's what's worrying you, let me put your mind at ease."

Kayleigh Jemison evidently had no compunction about taking a Louisville Slugger to his ego.

"We'll pay double, without the pretend fiancé thing. Final offer."

"Then no deal." She folded her arms. She'd gone from sheepish to defiant again. "The fiancé thing is nonnegotiable."

He'd thought she'd thrown that in as a bargaining chip just to get him to agree to double his original offer, but she was serious.

Dead serious.

"Then we'll pay one and a half times the assessed value and I'm sure one of my brothers would be happy enough to get a free vacation and play your fake fiancé for a week."

"Twice the value and *you* play fake fiancé for a week. Am I not being clear about this? Because I really feel like I am." She smirked, a hint of victory in her voice.

Parker ran a hand over his head and groaned.

"You're dreaming if you think I could even begin to pull this off. You know I was a terrible liar when we were kids. That hasn't changed."

"Then you'd better learn, Abbott."

"Why can't you take Max or Cole? Either of them would be thrilled to go on an all-expenses paid island vacation. I'm sure Cole would be more than happy to share a bed with you." His brother Cole, the one sibling who didn't help manage the distillery, seemed determined to sleep his way through half the town.

"No one said anything about sharing a bed. That's what makes you a pretend fiancé, *genius*." Kayleigh clenched her fists, her chest puffing out.

"You expect me to fake intimacy? We were friends

once, but we hardly know each other now. And you think I'll be able to pretend well enough to fool someone who was your close friend? You're being completely unreasonable here." Parker took a cloth from his pocket and cleaned his glasses. "Even for you, and that's saying a lot."

She sneered at him, then sighed. "You're right. We'd never fool Kira with this." She gestured between them. "She'd sense that we're virtual strangers."

Parker breathed a sigh of relief, returned his glasses to the bridge of his nose and picked up his pen again. "So in lieu of the whole pretend fiancé thing…"

"No in lieu of." Kayleigh shook her head vigorously and a few of her bouncy red curls spilled from the bandanna. "I didn't say we weren't doing it—I just said it wouldn't work the way things stand between us now. That means we need to put some effort into it. We have ten weeks to get to know each other."

"Kayleigh, how do you expect—"

"That's the deal, Abbott. Take it or leave it." Even the insidious grin slowly spreading across her face couldn't dim her beauty. If anything, the sly smile highlighted her perfect cheekbones.

Acquire this building, no matter what it takes.

He could hear his father's words in his head. When his siblings on the King's Finest board had laughed, insisting he wouldn't be able to cut a deal with Kayleigh Jemison, he'd taken it as a personal challenge.

Parker loved his mother and knew how much owning this piece of her family's history would mean to her. Still, it was a lot to ask.

His teeth clenched and one fist balled at his side. "I'll have the contract and confidentiality agreements drawn up and let you know when they're ready to be signed. For now, though, this deal stays between us."

Kayleigh could barely contain a grin as she gave him a two-finger salute. "Pleasure doin' business with you, Abbott."

Parker grunted in response as he headed to his car.

Now he was saddled with a broken-down building and a fake fiancée who hated his guts.

His siblings were going to get a kick out of this.

Three

"Are you all done?" Parker sat at one end of the conference-room table, fuming as his father, brothers Blake and Max, and sister, Zora, laughed so hard that tears came to their eyes. "If so, I'd like to get back to the business at hand."

"That Kayleigh is a shrewd businesswoman." His father dabbed his eyes with a hankie, then stuffed it into his pocket. "You have to give her that."

He could think of things he'd like to give Kayleigh Jemison. A compliment wasn't one of them.

She'd turned him into the family punch line and seemed determined to make the next few months of his life a nightmare. They still had to iron out the details, but he'd have to spend the next few months getting to know her. It'd be like two betta fish being placed in a single bowl.

"C'mon, Parker, don't try to act like you're not secretly looking forward to a little alone time with Kayleigh." Zora wiped away tears with her knuckle. "It's no secret you have a little—"

"I'm not and I don't." He addressed his sister—the baby of the family—pointedly. "Now, if we could get back to the details of the contract."

"Savannah won't believe it when I tell her this." Blake chuckled.

"Neither will Mom," Max added, shaking his head. "Once we finally tell her. But I'm sure the prospect of marrying off another one of her kids will thrill her to death."

"No one is getting married." Parker's voice came out shriller than he'd intended. He straightened his tie and released a slow breath. "I'm glad I could provide you all with a bit of amusement today, but we can finish this around the dinner table on Sunday." He tapped his Bvlgari Roma Finissimo watch. "Right now we're on the clock and I need to get the team's agreement on the details of this contract so I can get it revised and signed before Kayleigh changes her mind."

"Parker's right," his father said, with one final chuckle. "Time is of the essence. I think I speak for all of us when I say, we gladly accept Miss Jemison's terms."

Of course they did.

They weren't the ones sentenced to spend the next three months in hell.

* * *

"So, when were you going to tell me you proposed to Parker?" Savannah Abbott asked as Kayleigh slid into her seat in their favorite booth at the Magnolia Lake Bakery.

"First, I did *not* propose to Parker. Second, he said I wasn't permitted to talk to anyone about the deal, so I couldn't tell you."

"I had to hear it from Blake." Savannah's hazel eyes danced. "I thought it was an April Fools' joke."

Savannah was Parker Abbott's sister-in-law. When she'd come to town three years ago, she'd loathed the Abbotts as much as Kayleigh did. But while carrying out her plan to prove that half of the King's Finest Distillery rightfully belonged to her grandfather, Martin McDowell, Savannah had fallen for Blake Abbott. In the end it turned out that neither of their grandfathers had been completely honest about what had happened to their partnership all those years ago.

They'd both fessed up and Joseph Abbott had felt guilty enough to give McDowell and his two granddaughters—Savannah and her younger sister, Delaney—a share of the business. He'd also written Martin a seven-figure check.

"Honestly, I was kind of relieved that I couldn't tell you about my deal with Parker. It's embarrassing to admit that I needed to barter for a date to my friend's wedding."

"Why did you feel you needed to?" Savannah employed the same patient, soothing tone she used when trying to reason with her nearly two-year-old son, Davis.

"This isn't just any friend's wedding. She's my ex's younger sister."

"The guy you moved to Atlanta with after college?" Savannah looked up from sipping her coffee.

"Aidan." Kayleigh confirmed with a nod. "He's married now. To a gorgeous woman from the right family. Last I heard, they had a couple of kids together." Kayleigh gripped her mug tighter in response to the tightness in her chest.

"I'm starting to get the picture." Savannah squeezed her friend's hand. "But, sweetie, you were the one who walked away. You have nothing to prove to him or anyone else."

"I know, but the thought of being the only one there alone while everyone else on the island is boo'd up…" Kayleigh heaved a sigh and raked her fingers through her curls. "I couldn't bear for Aidan to look at me and feel like he dodged a bullet by not marrying me. Or worse, that he'd pity me."

"If he thinks that, he's a fool." Savannah gave her hand one last squeeze before picking up her mug and taking a sip of her vanilla decaf latte. "So I understand why you felt compelled to take someone as your date, but why Parker? I thought you couldn't stand him."

"I can't." Kayleigh's eyes met her friend's. She blew out a long breath. "But this was going to be awkward, no matter who I brought along. I figured that at least with Parker, I know exactly who I'm dealing with, so there won't be any misunderstandings. This is a business deal, not a hookup."

The corner of Savannah's mouth lifted in a smirk.

She brought the mug to her lips and mumbled under her breath, "If you say so."

"You don't actually think I *want* to spend an entire week sharing a room with Parker Abbott."

Savannah shrugged as she sipped her latte. "You two do have pretty passionate feelings for one another."

"It's pure, unadulterated loathing. Nothing more. Now can we change the subject?"

"After you answer a few more questions." Savannah set her cup down and leaned forward, folding her arms on the table. "Since you went for broke and declared that you were bringing your fiancé, won't it become painfully obvious that you two dislike each other?"

"Like I said, I may not have been thinking clearly." She shrugged. "I figured I'd put together a backstory of how we met. And we can fill out a couple of those questionnaires to get to know each other. You know the kind that ask about your favorite color and your ideal date?"

Savannah practically snorted. "*That's* your game plan?"

"Pretty much." Kayleigh's cheeks heated beneath her friend's stare. "I mean, we do have two and a half months to memorize this stuff."

"Kayleigh, sweetie…" Savannah took a deep breath as she returned her mug to the table. "Parker is supposed to be your fiancé, which means you two should look like you're head over heels in love. No basic questionnaire is going to get you two to that point. Not in a way that will convince anyone who spends more than three seconds with the two of you." Savannah sighed, but her hazel eyes were filled with warmth. "Are you sure that you should bring Parker on the trip? Can't you just say that your fiancé couldn't make it because of a business obligation?"

"It'll look like I made the whole thing up."

"Which you did."

"Sometimes a girl has to do what a girl has to do. You, of all people, should understand that." Kayleigh took a sip of her coffee.

Savannah's eyes widened and she lowered her gaze to her cup.

Kayleigh's cheeks stung and her gut twisted in a knot. "I'm sorry. I shouldn't have said that."

Savannah gave her a small nod, her eyes not meeting Kayleigh's.

Savannah and Blake had fallen in love and had managed to work things out, despite their rocky start. Still, Kayleigh knew her friend harbored guilt over the way she'd deceived Blake and his family in the beginning.

Kayleigh squeezed her friend's hand. "I didn't mean to sound bitchy and judgmental. I just thought that you'd understand that sometimes the ends justify the means. Your grandfather would never have gotten what was rightfully owed to him if it hadn't been for you. And he might never have rectified things with his old friend or gotten to see his great-grandson before he passed."

"I was trying to restore my grandfather's legacy and dig our family out of debt," Savannah said sharply. "I didn't do what I did just to make my ex jealous."

"Now who's being bitchy and judgmental?" Kayleigh raised a brow and drank the last of her coffee.

Savannah sighed. "This is important to you. I get it. But it still goes back to what I said before. You won't fool your ex or his sister with your sad little 'I love red and he loves green' routine."

"Then help me. Please." She flashed her best sad, puppy-dog eyes at her friend.

"Fine, but only if you'll do *exactly* what I say. I won't invest my time in this little scheme of yours if you're planning to half-ass it."

"Thank you, thank you, thank you!" Kayleigh bounced in her seat. "I'll do whatever you say. I promise. Parker on the other hand—"

"Don't worry about Parker." Savannah waved a hand dismissively. "Leave him to us." She pulled out her phone and opened her text app. "I'll enlist Blake and Benji to make sure Parker understands exactly what's at stake."

If Parker Abbott cared about her feelings, they'd still be friends.

Kayleigh's face burned and tears stung her eyes as she remembered the day in sixth grade when their friendship had ended. She'd caught Parker repeating things she'd confided in him about her father—the town drunk—to a chorus of laughter from the popular kids with whom he'd chosen to ingratiate himself.

"When do we start?"

"Right now." Savannah shoved a monogrammed pen and pad across the table. "Make a list of everything you like about Parker."

Kayleigh frowned. "Can't we start with something easier? Like a list of reasons he's incredibly irritating?"

"Do you want my help or not, Ms. Thing?"

Kayleigh pouted. "This is harder than I thought."

"You're not trying. Parker may be annoying, but he's brilliant. And he's determined when he believes he's right."

"Which is always," Kayleigh muttered. She jotted down *smart* and *determined*.

"You know, you and Parker have a lot in common."

"That's a low blow." Kayleigh dropped the pen. "Name one way I'm like Parker."

"You're both stubborn smart-asses who can be exasperating. You're both extremely good at what you do, and you're both carrying king-size chips on your shoulders."

"I said *one* thing." Kayleigh held up a finger. "The rest was completely unnecessary."

Savannah grinned. "Just keep working on that list. I'm going to grab something to eat. Want anything?"

Kayleigh shook her head as she studied the list.

She closed her eyes and pictured Parker's face. Beneath that constant scowl was a strong jaw, dark, piercing eyes and sensual lips framed by a neat, full goatee. Kayleigh's eyes opened suddenly as her cheeks flushed with heat.

Some women might find Parker hot—with or without his glasses.

She scribbled *fairly attractive*, *gainfully employed*, *wealthy* and *family-oriented*.

"You're making progress." Savannah set down a warm sticky bun and slid into her seat.

"Speaking of progress…doesn't that defeat the purpose of yoga this morning?"

"I'm allowed a few extra calories." Savannah broke into a slow grin and pressed a hand to her belly. "I'm pregnant."

"Savannah, that's wonderful!" Kayleigh hugged her friend.

She was thrilled for Savannah. She had the dream husband, a career she loved, an adorable little boy and another little one on the way. And she'd never have to worry about money again.

Still, Kayleigh envied her friend's happiness. Wanted a piece of it for herself.

"Thanks, but please don't tell anyone," Savannah said as they returned to their seats. "Blake and I will share the news with his family at dinner on Sunday. Then I'll call my sister."

"I won't say a word." Kayleigh forced a smile. "When is the baby due?"

"November." Savannah reviewed Kayleigh's list as she nibbled on the sticky bun. "This is a good start, but it's just the basics. And right now they're empty words. If you have any hope of pulling this off, you and Parker have to spend time getting to know each other."

The knot in Kayleigh's stomach tightened. "Are we talking about a couple of get-to-know-you sessions?"

"Sorry, babe." Savannah pushed her plate aside. Her grin indicated she wasn't sorry at all. "I'm talking full-on dating…on steroids."

"What's Option Two?" Kayleigh slumped in her seat. Her mouth went dry and her palms felt clammy.

"Tell your friend the truth. There is no fiancé and there never was one."

"Fine." Kayleigh dragged a hand across her forehead. "If you can convince Parker to do this, I'm in, too."

"Perfect." Savannah's Cheshire Cat grin faded. She placed a hand to her mouth. "I'm going to be sick."

Me, too. Kayleigh buried her forehead in her hand as her best friend made a beeline to the restroom.

Her saving grace was knowing Parker would never go for it.

Four

"Now you expect me to date Kayleigh Jemison, too? Have you all lost your freaking minds?" Parker paced the floor in the conference room. "It's bad enough I have to spend a week pretending to be her fiancé."

"You know this plan will never work the way things stand between you and Kayleigh now," Savannah said calmly. "Besides, it'll give you two a chance to finally hash things out."

"Your sister-in-law is right, son," Duke piped up. "This feud between you two has gone on for too long."

"It isn't a feud," Parker clarified. "She hates my guts. End of story."

"You hurt her, Parker, and you never even apologized," his sister pointed out. "What do you expect?"

"For the hundredth time… I didn't say anything she hadn't said herself."

"I love you, Park," his sister said. "But you can be an asshole sometimes. You're so determined to prove yourself right that you're not giving the slightest consideration to Kayleigh's feelings."

"Let's not stoop to name-calling, baby girl," their father said sternly, glancing around the room at all of them.

He came to stand beside Parker in front of the conference room windows and placed a hand on his shoulder.

"Son, I realize that I'm asking a lot of you, but this is important to me because it's important to your mother. She's put her heart and soul into supporting my father's dream and into raising this family. This is our chance to help her revive her father's legacy. It's something she's dreamed about for years, and now we finally have the opportunity to make it happen. I'm sorry that the bulk of the load will fall to you. But this is important, Parker. Not just for your mother, but for King's Finest, too."

Parker groaned as he stared out the window. They had no idea what they were asking of him.

Kayleigh Jemison loathed him, but despite what his family believed, he didn't despise her. He was angry with Kayleigh. Maybe even hurt by her unrelenting disdain. But spending time with her at Blake and Savannah's wedding had made it clear that he was still very fond of her.

Being forced to spend a week with Kayleigh would test his will in more ways than they knew.

"I'll do it for Mom." Parker nodded. "And for the sake of this deal."

His father clapped a hand on his back and smiled. "Thank you, son. This means a lot to all of us."

His father was counting on him. Hell, his entire family was counting on him to make this deal happen. He'd been given a gift. He wanted to prove that when it was time to name a successor to the King's Finest throne, he was the obvious choice. What better way to show his fitness for the role of CEO than by proving that he'd go beyond the call of duty to ensure the company's success?

Their receptionist, Lianna, called the conference room to announce the arrivals of Kayleigh and their attorney, Lane Dennings.

"Speak now or forever hold your peace." Max could barely contain his grin as Blake and Zora dissolved into laughter in response to his marriage pun.

Parker wouldn't give his siblings the satisfaction of reacting. He simply ignored them.

"Ready, son?" His father held back a smile.

Parker nodded and sat at the table.

"I'll clear the room. Go ahead and send them up, Lianna," his father said. "I'll meet them at the elevator."

"You're putting us out?" Zora groused.

"We don't want to intimidate her. Parker, Lane and I have to be here, and Kayleigh requested that Savannah stay."

"Well, I'm going down to the day care to spend some time with Davis before I go back to work." Blake looked especially happy. He leaned down and gave his wife a quick kiss before exiting on the heels of Max, Zora and their father.

"Right this way, ladies," his father was saying.

Parker's eyes met Kayleigh's as she entered the room. His pulse quickened and his mouth went dry.

He'd expected her to show up in tattered jeans and a T-shirt, with her hair a mess. But she hadn't.

Kayleigh was stunning in a simple white blouse and a plain black skirt with a hemline that hovered just above her knees. Her hair fell below her shoulders in bouncy curls that swayed with every movement.

He'd barely managed spending a single day with her when he'd been charged with escorting her down the aisle at Blake and Savannah's wedding.

Ten weeks and ten dates?

He was an absolute goner.

Kayleigh Jemison was not easily intimidated. But there was something unnerving about Parker Abbott's appraisal as she entered the conference room.

His eyes widened with surprise as his gaze met hers and then slowly trailed down the length of her body.

Savannah had been right. Dressing the part was a good choice. It'd thrown Parker for a loop.

What she hadn't expected was that she'd find his reaction unsettling. Her cheeks felt warm and there was a fluttering low in her belly.

Parker scrambled to his feet and buttoned the heather-gray suit jacket that fit him so well. He offered a stern nod.

Kayleigh returned the gesture before turning her attention to Duke Abbott, who stood beside his son.

"Ladies, please have a seat." Duke gestured toward

the chair beside Savannah. "Kayleigh, thank you for agreeing to meet us here."

She smoothed down the black A-line skirt that skimmed her thighs before taking her seat next to her friend, who squeezed her arm reassuringly. "Thank you for agreeing to my price and terms."

Kayleigh insisted that the purchase agreement for her building clearly spell out that the deal was contingent on Parker fulfilling his end of the bargain. Duke agreed readily, assuring her that he was a man of his word, as was Parker.

In her experience, neither Duke nor his son were trustworthy. But she needed both of them for now, so she'd play nice.

"I appreciate your willingness to accommodate my unusual request." Kayleigh tucked her hair behind her ears to keep it from falling forward.

Parker cleared his throat. "Ready to sign the contract?"

"My attorney went over the agreement thoroughly, but I'd prefer to schedule the ten agreed-upon dates *prior* to signing the agreement."

A deep frown creased Parker's forehead. He opened his leather-bound planner. "For the sake of simplicity, why don't we make it the same day and time each week?"

"What if we already have an event planned that day?"

Parker shrugged. "Then we make that our 'date.'" He used air quotes.

Kayleigh wasn't looking forward to combing through

her calendar to schedule ten dates with Parker Abbott any more than he seemed to be.

"That's a reasonable way to settle this, but I think we should allow for flexibility on the time of the 'date.'" She used air quotes, too.

Parker grunted his agreement without looking up.

"How about Sunday afternoons?" she offered.

"We have our family dinner on Sundays." Parker frowned. "How about Wednesday evenings?"

"In the middle of the week?" Now it was Kayleigh's turn to frown. "That's when I do most of my metal-work, and I'm in the studio pretty late, so that won't work for me."

Parker stared up from his datebook. "Saturday afternoons?"

"I can make Saturday work." Kayleigh opened the calendar app on her phone. She'd gotten some part-time help on the weekends; otherwise she would've had to work on Saturday afternoons.

Parker stroked his goatee as he contemplated the calendar. Kayleigh couldn't help studying his handsome features. Neat, thick brows framed his pensive, dark eyes. Full, kissable lips tugged down in an ever-present frown. His slim-cut gray suit accentuated his long, lean frame.

Okay, so she could definitely see why some women might consider Parker Abbott's handsome-geek-chic look hot.

"How long will these dates be?" Parker skipped the air quotes this time, but his tone indicated that they were implied.

"We should allow for flexibility, but two to three hours on average should give us time to rehearse our story and get to know each other."

"Agreed." Parker made careful notes in his datebook. "How do we decide what we'll do on each date?"

"We'll take turns choosing." Kayleigh shrugged.

"Seems fair." Parker nodded. "Why don't you choose first?"

"Actually, I have a suggestion for your first date," Savannah interjected.

They both turned toward her.

"Blake and I want you to come to our house. Nothing fancy, just homemade pizza and a friendly board game or two, after we iron out your story."

"Story?" The lines in Parker's forehead deepened.

"How you two met, why you fell in love with her, your plans for the wedding. The kinds of questions that Kayleigh's friend and her—" Savannah paused when Kayleigh frowned and subtly shook her head "—family are sure to ask."

"I have an excellent memory." Parker tapped his temple.

"It's not about repeating data verbatim, Parker." Savannah was remarkably patient with him. Perhaps because she was the only person in the room accustomed to managing the whims of a toddler. "You must be convincing when you say it."

Parker didn't acknowledge Savannah's statement, but he didn't object either. In Kayleigh's book, that was progress.

"Besides, it's a low-stress way for you two to ease into this arrangement," Savannah added.

"Sounds reasonable." Parker jotted the appointment down in his book. "What time should we be there?"

After the time was set, Duke stepped in to move the process along. He reiterated that the confidentiality agreement prevented her from discussing the deal with anyone other than Savannah or the six members of the King's Finest executive board: Duke, Blake, Parker, Max, Zora and founder Joseph Abbott. She wasn't even permitted to discuss the arrangement with his wife, Iris. Though they wouldn't share the details of the project, it was to be a surprise for her.

"Won't she wonder why Parker and I are suddenly spending so much time together?" Kayleigh frowned.

"She's always hoped that you two would try and repair your friendship." Savannah smiled warmly. "So, as far as Iris is concerned, this is Project Friendship."

Kayleigh had zero interest in trying to resurrect a friendship that had been in tatters for far longer than it had existed. But if that would make Iris feel better, fine.

Once the paperwork was signed, Kayleigh shook Duke's hand, then Parker's.

There was something in his firm handshake and piercing gaze that sent a shiver down her spine. She hugged Savannah and quickly excused herself, eager to make her way back to her Jeep. When she did, she sank into the driver's seat and leaned against the headrest.

Had she really been ogling Parker Abbott? And had he been doing the same?

No, of course not. She despised Parker and he obviously felt the same way about her. It wasn't attraction; it was nerves, plain and simple. She'd insisted on Parker being the one to escort her to Kira's wedding because with him there would be no blurring of the lines. She could count on Parker to keep their dealings strictly business. And she needed to do the same.

Ten dates, then one week together on the island. Afterward they'd both walk away with exactly what they wanted.

Negotiating the deal had been the easy part. Getting to know each other well enough to make Kira and her family believe they were a couple in love and engaged to be married…that was the hard part.

But she'd do it, no matter what. Because the looks of pity she'd garner from her ex and his family if she arrived alone were something she simply couldn't endure.

Five

Kayleigh pulled into Blake and Savannah's driveway and parked her mud-spattered Jeep beside Parker's pristine blue BMW. She wasn't sure how he managed it, but the rims always gleamed and the car always looked like it had just rolled out of the car wash.

Kayleigh studied the gorgeous, timber-frame home situated on a lake.

Parker was right; the Abbotts were on an entirely different spectrum than she was. She had a little shop, one part-time employee and a vehicle that was well over ten years old.

As she stepped out of the Jeep, her legs felt unsteady.

She hated to admit it, even to herself, but she was genuinely nervous about this first date with Parker. It was less of a date and more of a strategic-planning session. But that didn't stop the fluttery feeling in her stomach or the zing of electricity that trailed down her spine when she remembered how their palms had touched when he'd shaken her hand. Or the heat in his dark eyes as he'd surveyed her in her little black skirt.

It was Parker Abbott, for God's sake. The man she'd spent most of her life despising. She needed to get a grip.

"Kayleigh." Savannah stood in the doorway on their large front porch, with Davis on her hip. Her smile was broad and welcoming.

A little of the tension in Kayleigh's shoulders eased as she allowed her friend to give her a hug.

Davis giggled in response to Kayleigh's customary greeting of tickling his belly.

Savannah put the toddler down and instructed him to go to his father, who was in the great room with his Uncle Parker.

Kayleigh's spine stiffened at the mention of Parker's name, but she forced a smile as she faced her friend.

Savannah practically glowed. Her bouncy curls were shiny and radiant. Her hazel eyes seemed to be lit from within.

"One more day before your secret's out," Kayleigh whispered conspiratorially as she glanced down at her friend's belly.

Savannah's hand went there instinctively. "I know. It's been killing us to keep the news to ourselves."

"What news?" Parker appeared suddenly in the kitchen.

"What can I get you, Parker?" Savannah's tone made it clear that she wouldn't be answering his question.

He shook his glass, filled with ice. "Came to get water, but I've got it. Thanks." He nodded toward her. "Hello, Kayleigh."

"Parker." She nodded back.

There was an uncomfortable pause.

"And this is why we need to practice." Savannah glanced from Kayleigh to Parker and back. "Are you sure we shouldn't try for two dates per week, or maybe three?"

"No!" They both said, simultaneously.

"We're both very busy, so it'd be difficult to find the time." Parker looked the tiniest bit apologetic.

"Absolutely," Kayleigh agreed. "We'll make the time we've already allotted work. Besides, with your help, we'll do fine."

The slightest smile curved one edge of Parker's mouth.

Kayleigh followed her friend to the great room, satisfied with having been the reason for a genuine Parker Abbott smile.

Dinner was remarkable. They fell into an easy, comfortable rhythm. Blake and Savannah went out of their way to keep the conversation flowing, expertly drawing them in and looking for ways to get them talking to each other.

"All right," Savannah said, when Blake took Davis upstairs to give him a bath before bed. "Take out your lists."

Parker opened his datebook while Kayleigh pulled the wrinkled, coffee-stained sheet of paper from her pocket.

"Read them to each other." Savannah beamed.

Kayleigh clutched the wrinkled sheet of paper. "You want me to read it to him? Out loud?"

"Yes," Savannah said resolutely. "Remember, this is a list of all the reasons you truly admire each other. We'll use them to craft the story of how you two fell in love."

"I'll go first." There was a beat of silence as Parker pushed his glasses up the bridge of his nose. He turned his body toward hers, but his gaze didn't leave the page. "I admire Kayleigh's sense of compassion, her determination, her courage and her creativity." He glanced up at her finally. "I also appreciate her unique beauty."

Arms folded, Kayleigh bristled at the term *unique beauty*. Was that his way of saying she had a face that only a mother could love? More important, even if it was Parker's attempt at a backhanded compliment, why should she care what Parker thought of her?

Probably for the same reason she cared about what the Brennans thought of her. She'd spent so much of her life unable to control the narrative about herself and her family. Had been called "poor little thing" either directly or by adults whispering in grocery aisles who didn't think she'd heard them. So now she managed as much of other people's perception about her as she could and convinced herself she didn't care in the instances when she couldn't.

"That's a great list, Parker." Savannah seemed to sense her uneasiness. "But let's get more specific about why you admire those qualities in Kayleigh."

Her face felt hot and her eyes widened as she met

Parker's gaze. His cheeks and forehead flushed; he looked as panicked by the prospect as she felt.

This could go sideways fast.

Parker was sure his heart was attempting to beat its way out of his chest as his eyes met Kayleigh's. She'd narrowed her gaze and folded her arms when he'd described her beauty as *unique*. So though he'd meant it as a compliment, she obviously hadn't taken it that way.

Strike one.

He opened his mouth to launch into an explanation of how she'd misunderstood him again, but Benji's advice to him over drinks with the guys the night before echoed in his head.

Don't be a jackass.

Max had suggested that he make it his motto and tattoo it on the inside of his wrist, if need be.

Parker swallowed hard and held Kayleigh's gaze. "I like that she demonstrates compassion through volunteering and activism. I admire the courage it must've taken to start her own business and keep it going."

Kayleigh's arms relaxed and her gaze softened. She seemed stunned that he could string together a complete sentence that didn't inadvertently insult her.

"Her creativity is evident in the jewelry pieces she designs, and her unique style sets her apart from anyone else I've ever known." He dropped his gaze from hers for a moment. "And she's gorgeous. But in a way that makes her stand out as different. Which I appreciate."

When Parker was done, neither Savannah nor Kayleigh spoke. They exchanged looks and then stared at him again.

Had he screwed up again?

"Was that bad?" he asked his sister-in-law.

"No, Parker. It wasn't. It was beautiful." She beamed at him with an expression similar to the one she employed whenever his young nephew acquired some new skill.

"Kayleigh, how about you? What do you admire about Parker?"

Kayleigh silently consulted her wrinkled, stained sheet of paper again before raising her eyes to meet his. She adjusted in her chair, sitting taller.

"Parker is brilliant. He excels in math, science, business and just about anything he puts his mind to. I admire his focused determination and his commitment to his family and their business." Kayleigh ran her fingers through the long, curly ponytail hanging over one shoulder. "He's tall, but not too tall. And handsome, despite always scowling. Oh, and I like the goatee. It suits him."

Savannah looked up from the notes she was scribbling. "I'm gonna check on the boys and let Benny and Sam out. Why don't you two go over your lists again, but this time I want you to speak directly to each other. Be back in a sec."

Parker frowned. Maybe this was Savannah's way of getting a little payback from the time he'd been hell-bent on having her tossed in jail because he thought she was stealing from the King's Finest archives.

"I'll go first again," he said, finally.

"One more thing," Savannah called from above as she leaned over the railing. "Hold hands this time."

"What?" Kayleigh looked up at her friend.

"Why?" Parker asked simultaneously.

"You don't expect to spend an entire week pretending to be engaged without a little hand-holding or an affectionate kiss or two, do you? Hate to break it to you, puddin', but that's part of the sell. So…" She clapped. "Again. Holding hands. Like you mean it. Let's go!"

And that was why Savannah was such a good fit for their family and business. She'd never been intimidated by what people perceived as his perpetual grouchiness. And she'd never been afraid to challenge him or anyone else in their family, including his father and grandfather.

"I hadn't thought of that," Kayleigh muttered, more to herself than him. "With this emotional distance between us…there's no point in even doing this."

Was she calling the whole thing off? Because that was an idea he could get behind, even if it meant paying a little more for her building. "So does that mean—"

"No, you're not off the hook, Abbott." She sighed, then rose to her feet and faced him, her hand extended.

Parker wiped his palms on his pants legs and stood, too. He placed his much larger hand in her outstretched one.

Her skin was soft and warm and he inhaled her subtle vanilla scent that reminded him of buttercream frosting.

Kayleigh met his gaze. "Parker, I admire your intelligence, your focused determination and ability to see the endgame when everyone else is just getting suited up. I love how close you are to your family. You obviously love them. And…" She sighed softly. "You're very handsome—with or without your glasses."

"Thanks, Kayleigh." He tightened his grip on her

hand. "I admire your strength and tenacity. When you have a goal in mind, you don't let anything stop you, not even your own fears. I admire the creativity required to take what's essentially scrap metal and a few rocks and turn it into something…magnificent. And I love that you have your own sense of style. You own your unique beauty instead of buying into someone else's."

Kayleigh stared at him with surprise and then thanked him.

"Not bad, you two." Blake carried Davis downstairs in his cartoon-character pajamas, with Savannah on his heels.

"Thanks," Kayleigh muttered, yanking her hand from Parker's and stepping away. As if they'd been caught making out.

He shoved his hands in his pockets, his cheeks warm.

"Little Man wanted to say good-night to Uncle Parker and Aunt Kayleigh." Blake looked at his son proudly.

"Good night, Davis." Kayleigh tickled the boy's belly and kissed his cheek. For a moment Parker was envious of little Davis as he squirmed and giggled in response.

"Good night, Little Man." Parker mussed the boy's soft curls. "See you tomorrow at Grammie and Grandpa's house."

Davis called good-night to them repeatedly as his father carried him up to bed.

"That wasn't too hard, now was it?" Savannah grinned. "No one died, and the earth is still spinning on its axis."

"You didn't say you'd be listening." Kayleigh jabbed the air with an accusatory finger.

"Didn't say I wouldn't, either." Savannah shrugged. "I just thought you'd both feel less self-conscious without observers."

"Though clearly we had an audience." Parker pushed his glasses up the bridge of his nose.

"As you will at the wedding," she reminded them. "So you need to be able to say it like you mean it, whether it's in front of two people or two hundred."

Parker was a straightforward kind of guy who said what he meant, even if people sometimes misconstrued his words. Putting on a show for Kayleigh's old friend didn't sit well with him.

If they were *really* friends, she should be able to tell the woman the truth without judgment. But then he certainly hadn't been a shining example of how a good friend behaved, had he?

"I doubt we'll need to pull this shtick in front of many people. No one but Kira and her immediate family will care."

"Still, it's better to be prepared." Savannah nodded toward him. "Since Parker looks a little green, I'd suggest you try again until you can both recite the words comfortably. When you're done, there'll be cake." She winked.

Parker turned toward Kayleigh and extended his hand. "We'd better try a few more times before the overlord comes back."

"I heard that!" Savannah called.

"We wanted you to!" Kayleigh responded.

Parker couldn't help smiling as Kayleigh put her hand in his.

Six

Kayleigh pulled her flame-red Jeep, with the hardtop removed, into Parker's driveway. He glanced down at the fancy sports watch on his wrist and frowned as he rolled his mountain bike out of the garage. He was wearing a black long-sleeve sports shirt that revealed a more impressive chest and biceps than she'd have expected of the pencil pusher. His black mountain-biking pants had a loose fit but highlighted his strong legs and surprisingly impressive hindquarters.

Not that she cared.

"You're late," Parker groused, as if she wasn't already aware.

She bit back her smart-ass comeback as she hopped out of the truck and met him at the back, where her bicycle was strapped onto the bike rack. "Danette needed help locating one of the orders that had to be shipped out today."

"Don't you have some sort of organizing system to keep from losing orders?" Parker lifted his bicycle and strapped it onto the rack and she secured it.

She nodded toward his garage—organized with high-end cabinetry on one wall and a paneled system of shelves, hooks and baskets on the opposite and back walls. "I'm clearly not as organized as you are."

"Organization is the key to efficiency." Parker opened the passenger door and nearly jumped out of his skin when her three-year-old golden retriever, Cricket, barked from her perch in the front seat of the truck.

"Are you afraid of dogs?" Kayleigh strapped on her seat belt. "Is that why Blake and Savannah kept poor Benny and Sam in the den while we were there last week?"

"I'm not afraid of Benny and Sam." He seemed insulted by the question. "I'm just not a big fan of keeping pets indoors."

Parker folded his arms and stared at Cricket, who growled at him disapprovingly. "Is he gonna move?"

"*She* called shotgun on the ride over, so that's a no, chief." Kayleigh grinned before breaking into laughter at his look of outrage. "I'm just kidding, Abbott. Geez, relax. You look like you're about to crap a diamond."

Parker's eyes widened, then narrowed as he stared at her.

Kayleigh kissed Cricket's nose and petted her head. "Go to the back seat, girl. It'll be all right. Despite the mean mug, Parker here is relatively harmless."

Cricket climbed onto the back seat begrudgingly and

barked again to make sure Parker understood how displeased she was.

He dusted bits of Cricket's hair from the front seat before getting in and using a phone app to close his garage door.

"Thanks for the ride," Parker said after a few minutes on the road together in silence.

"You obviously weren't going to put a bike rack on the back of that shiny Beamer. I didn't have much of an option if I wanted you to come along." She stared ahead at the road. "Nice bike. How often do you ride?"

"My family bought it one year for my birthday." He shrugged. "Every now and then, one of my brothers decides we all need to go riding. Usually it's Cole."

That explained it. Parker didn't seem like the kind of guy who hit the bike trail regularly, though he certainly looked the part in his expensive gear.

"Honestly, I think the outdoors is overrated. I never fared very well trekking in the woods with my brothers as a kid." He absently grazed the scar she knew he had just above his knee from when he'd tumbled down a hill as a boy. "And then, of course, there's my schedule."

"I hate to break it to you, but camping is on the agenda in a few weeks. I planned the trip months ago, but you said that if we already had something on the books—"

"I know, I know." Parker clearly regretted that decision.

"Do you have a tent and camping gear?"

"Wait…you mean old-school camping? As in sleeping on the ground rather than in a cabin or RV?"

"My dad loved camping, and we always roughed it." Her lips curved in an involuntary smile. Those annual family camping trips were the highlight of her childhood. "Since I've been back home, I kind of keep up the tradition."

"Oh." Parker cleared his throat. "I never got a chance to say how sorry I was about the loss of your dad and then your mom. She was a really sweet lady, and she had an amazing smile. Same as yours."

"Thank you." Kayleigh's chest felt heavy.

"Since it's a family tradition, is Evvy coming, too?"

"No." Kayleigh's back tensed. Her strained relationship with her older sister, Evelisse, was another sensitive topic.

"I haven't seen Evvy since—"

"My mother's funeral," Kayleigh said sharply.

"Where does she live now?"

"She got a job in LA after college. Been there ever since."

"You adored Evvy when we were kids. What changed?"

"I realize you don't always pick up on body language, Parker, so I'll be direct." She managed to keep her voice even, despite her irritation. "I do *not* want to talk about my sister."

"We're supposed to be engaged," he muttered. "Seems like something a fiancé would know."

Now he wants to be helpful.

"Fine." Kayleigh heaved a sigh. "Evvy is desperate to erase our family's past history. She's still embarrassed about our dad. Ashamed of how poor we were growing up. She doesn't want any part of this town or anything that reminds her of the humiliation she endured here."

"Does that include you?"

She gripped the wheel so tightly, her knuckles ached. "It would seem so."

"I'm sorry, Kayleigh." Parker spoke after a long, uncomfortable pause. "I honestly didn't know."

"Well, now you do. So let's not talk about it anymore."

Cricket growled at Parker and then barked twice.

"Seems your dog doesn't want me to talk about it anymore either," Parker muttered.

"Her name is Cricket, and she's an excellent judge of character."

"Meaning?"

"She senses how anxious you are around her, which is why she distrusts you. And she senses how anxious you're making me. As you can see, she doesn't like it."

Parker glanced over his shoulder at Cricket. "Has it been scientifically proven that dogs can sense emotions, or are you basing this on anecdotal evidence?"

"It's a real thing, professor. Google it or something." Kayleigh rolled her eyes and sighed. She just wanted to get through the day without attempting to strangle Parker Abbott. That was looking less likely with each passing minute. "Maybe we should try for some meaningless small talk."

"All right. Maybe you could tell me why we're *really* doing this pretend fiancé thing?"

Parker obviously didn't understand the concept of small talk.

"I don't want to be the only person going solo at a romantic-destination wedding." She kneaded the Parker-induced knot forming in her neck. "I already explained this."

"You *implied* it," he clarified. "But I'm not buying it."

"Why not?" Kayleigh hit a bump in the road intentionally. Parker could use a good jostling.

"You don't usually care what other people think. Especially not enough to go through such an elaborate ruse."

Parker knew her better than she thought.

"And last week, Savannah was about to say something, but you cut her off. You obviously didn't want me to know."

"Then why are you asking about it?"

"I'm being forced to jump through a flaming hoop like a trained poodle. Don't you think I deserve to know whose benefit I'm doing it for?"

Actually, she didn't.

But Parker was as stubborn as she was. He wouldn't let this go, so she might as well level with him.

"The bride-to-be is my ex's younger sister."

"You're doing this for some guy?" He sounded profoundly disappointed in her for being so shallow.

"He's not just any guy. He was going to ask me to marry him."

"He was your *actual* fiancé?" Parker turned his body toward hers.

"I didn't give him a chance to ask," she said tersely.

"Why not?"

"I loved him. Very much. Maybe if the circumstances between us had been different—"

"Different how?"

"The Brennans are a wealthy, old-money Irish family. Part of the Atlanta aristocracy with the storied sugar plantation to prove it." Kayleigh shifted gears as they climbed into steeper terrain.

"And?" Parker seemed genuinely perplexed as to why any of that made a difference.

"His mother wasn't keen on the idea of a brown-skinned girl with no family or fortune to speak of making her way onto the illustrious Brennan family tree."

Parker's hands curled into fists on his lap. "If that's the kind of people they are, you made the right decision not to marry into their family."

"Don't get me wrong, she was never overt about it. And don't get the wrong impression of Kira or Aidan. Neither of them is like that. So much so that I don't think either of them recognized it in their mother."

"Do you regret not marrying Aidan?" Parker asked after a few moments of awkward silence between them.

"It was the right choice for both of us." Kayleigh shrugged, trying to shut out the painful memories of the decision she'd made that day. "He got married a couple years later. Last I heard they were happily married with two kids."

"And you?" His tone was softer.

Kayleigh focused on the road ahead. She couldn't bear to see the same pity in Parker's eyes that she heard in his voice.

"I'm better off without the hassle. Now story time is over. Unless you want to see Cricket do a mean imitation of an attack dog, I suggest we steer the conversation away from all of my failed relationships."

Cricket growled in response, and a smile slowly crept across Kayleigh's face.

Good girl, Cricket. Good girl.

* * *

Parker pulled out a cloth and cleaned his glasses without responding. He was reasonably sure Kayleigh was joking, but with her growling dog in the back seat, who obviously wasn't a fan, it seemed better not to test the limits.

Still, he felt a sense of satisfaction at getting Kayleigh to open up to him a little. When they were kids, she'd talked to him about everything, especially her family.

He'd missed those conversations and the easy friendship they'd once shared.

He glanced over at Kayleigh. His eyes were drawn to her strong, toned thighs, visible in her distressed, cut-off denim shorts, which were about an inch and a half too long to be considered Daisy Dukes. Her fitted baseball tee highlighted her ample breasts, and the deep vee offered a peek of her cleavage.

Not that he was looking. He just happened to be a very observant guy who noticed things.

Parker glanced around at the rugged terrain. "We're biking in the mountains?"

"You've got a pricey mountain bike and hard-core biker gear. Don't you want to put it to good use?"

Not particularly.

He ignored her question. "Do you often ride up here?"

"As often as I can. Savannah's ridden up here with me a few times. But it looks like we won't be doing that anytime soon." Kayleigh pulled into a parking lot for the mountain trail. "I hear you're going to be an uncle again."

"Seems that way," he said absently, studying the trail

up ahead and calculating whether he'd brought enough water.

"If you're not up to this, we can take the beginner trail," she offered.

He hadn't been sure what possessed his family to purchase the bicycle in the first place. It certainly wasn't his ideal way to spend an afternoon. But he'd accepted the gift gratefully and gone for a ride with them whenever the occasion arose.

As much as he wanted to accept Kayleigh's offer to bike an easier trail instead, there was no way he'd give her the satisfaction of believing that he was incapable of tackling a trail that she and Savannah managed without difficulty.

"No, this is fine." Parker frowned, stepping out of the truck.

Kayleigh hopped out, opened the back door for Cricket and pulled out a backpack. She put it on as she watched him take his cycle down from the rack.

Kayleigh reached for her bike, but he engaged his kickstand, then took the bike down for her.

"Thanks." Kayleigh grabbed the handlebar and seat. Her hand accidentally brushed his and she quickly withdrew it, as if her skin had been burned. She glanced up at him momentarily, cheeks flushed.

Parker ignored the zing of electricity he felt when her skin touched his. The same sensation that had crawled up his arm when he'd shaken her hand at the office, the day she'd signed the deal.

"How are you going to manage her while you're riding?" Parker nodded toward Cricket, who gave him her death stare.

Kayleigh indicated the metal bar extending from her seat. An extendable leash was attached to it.

"Clever." He watched as she connected it to Cricket's collar, then patted the dog's side.

Kayleigh strapped on her helmet and mounted the bicycle. The position drew his attention to her generous bottom.

Good Georgia peach.

Heat prickled his cheeks, and his face suddenly felt hot, despite the cool, early spring temperature.

"Everything okay?" She stared at him, her eyebrows drawn.

"Yes, of course." He put on his helmet and gloves, then mounted his bicycle, too.

"We'll take the easier of the two mountain trails," Kayleigh called over her shoulder as she rode toward it.

"Not necessary. Whatever you do normally is fine."

"You're sure?" Kayleigh didn't sound convinced.

"Positive."

"All right." She changed direction and headed toward the entrance of the advanced trail.

It was his second big mistake of the day.

"Parker, are you sure you don't want to go back?" Kayleigh stopped her bike and put one foot on the ground after they'd been riding for about forty minutes.

"I'm...good," he coughed, barely able to get the words out. Sweat ran down his face and stung his eyes.

"God, you look like you're about to pass out." Kayleigh put the kickstand down and hopped off her bike, looking alarmed. "Your face is red, you're practically hyperventilating and I'm pretty sure you're melting."

"It's no big deal. I'm fine."

"You are *not* passing out on me." She pointed a finger at him. "I'll leave your ass up here—I swear. You're too damned heavy to carry back down that hill. Get off the bike and sit down for a while." She indicated a wooden picnic table. "You brought water, didn't you?"

He nodded, still trying to catch his breath while Kayleigh wasn't even breathing heavily. Parker collapsed on the bench, took out a bottle of water and downed it.

Kayleigh poured water in her hand for Cricket to drink, then sat next to him on the bench, finishing the bottle off.

"I didn't consider how tough this trail is for someone who isn't very physical. We should've stayed on flat terrain."

"What do you mean someone who isn't physical?" He frowned, opening another bottle of water.

"I mean you spend most of your day at a desk. Physical labor isn't your thing, and there's nothing wrong with that. We've all got limitations."

"I'm fine." Parker stood quickly, his head spinning a little from the sudden movement. He wavered and she reached out to steady him. She pulled him down on the bench beside her and his thigh grazed hers.

"You are not fine, and I don't want to be the one who has to explain to your parents that you died on the side of this mountain because you didn't want to be shown up by a girl. Seriously, Parker, we're not ten. Get over the chauvinist bullshit."

He was more embarrassed by her accusation than he had been by his inability to keep up with her on the trail.

Don't be a jackass.

Kayleigh was right. He'd gone soft. He spent most of his day sitting behind a desk and it showed.

From the look of her toned body and the endurance she'd shown on the trail despite the steep inclines, Kayleigh Jemison was no stranger to physicality. Parker swallowed hard, heat spreading through his face and chest at the thought.

"You didn't do badly, this being your first time." Kayleigh nudged him with her elbow and smiled.

"Thanks." He drank more water. His breathing finally slowed enough for him to speak normally.

He was melting in the hot sun like the Wicked Witch in *The Wizard of Oz.* Meanwhile Kayleigh glowed, with a light sheen on her forehead and chest, and smelled like sunshine and vanilla.

She reached into her backpack and handed him a protein bar. "It tastes like cardboard coated with peanut butter and chocolate, but it'll give you enough fuel to get back down the trail."

Parker accepted it gratefully, opened the package and took a bite. She'd been generous with her description of the taste. But if it would give him a boost of much-needed energy, he'd eat three of the damn things. "How often do you bike this mountain?"

"Every chance I get. It's a good place to enjoy the peace and quiet and get out of my own head. Forget whatever is bothering me."

"Like?"

"You wouldn't understand." Kayleigh gave Cricket

the last of her bottle of water, then tossed all of the empties into a nearby recycling bin.

She put her backpack back on and walked over to her bike.

"Why wouldn't I understand?" He sat on his bike and released the kickstand.

"Because…you're one of the Mighty Abbotts. You guys don't have real-people problems." Her tone was sharp.

"That's not fair, Kayleigh. I've never purported to be better than you or anyone else."

"You don't have to say it. It's evident in how you deal with people. In how your father treated my mother when he lowballed her on that property you all expanded on. Or how you walked into my shop with your nose in the air, like you had a right to my property, whether I wanted to sell it or not."

"My father doesn't lowball people. He pays everyone a fair price. He always has. And we were more than generous with you, despite your unorthodox request. After all I'm here, aren't I?"

There was sadness in her brown eyes. "Then I guess I should be grateful, huh?"

Kayleigh took off down the trail on her bike, without waiting for his response.

Dammit.

Parker groaned as he followed Kayleigh and Cricket back down the hill, hoping she wouldn't decide that leaving him on that mountain to die was a pretty good idea after all.

Seven

Kayleigh parked her truck on the grass, along with the cars of the other friends and family members who'd been invited to Duke and Iris's place for a joint birthday party for Blake and Savannah's son Davis, who'd turned two and Benji and Sloane's twins, Beau and Bailey, who'd turned one.

Every muscle in her body was tense, her heart raced and her stomach was twisted in knots. The last thing she'd wanted to do was step foot in the lair of the devil himself, Duke Abbott. Sitting across from him at a conference table when she'd clearly had the upper hand was one thing. Stepping inside his home and playing nice at a social gathering was something else altogether.

She wanted to start up the Jeep, turn around and

leave. Make some excuse as to why she couldn't stay. But this was her and Parker's fifth date. More important, Savannah had enlisted her to do crafts with the children. It was a service she'd intended to add to her business menu, and this was the perfect chance to promote her newest offering.

Kayleigh got out of the truck and hauled her case of art supplies out of the back seat while also struggling to retrieve all three birthday gifts.

"Can I help you?"

The husky, sensual voice startled her. She quickly stood up straight and turned around.

"Cole Abbott." Kayleigh folded her arms. "You were staring at my ass, weren't you?"

His sensual lips curled in a smirk. "You looked like you were struggling, but if you'd rather carry everything in yourself—"

"No, I could use your help." She chose to ignore his nonanswer; instead she handed him the stack of colorfully wrapped gifts.

She grabbed her purse and the art case, then followed Cole to the front door of the grand home. The exterior was made of gray stacked stone and shakes made of poplar bark. The house overlooked the gorgeous Smoky Mountains.

Cole studied the exterior as if he was critiquing the home his company had built.

Kayleigh scanned the structure. "You do amazing work, Cole. This place is incredible, and the views must be breathtaking."

"You've never been here?" Cole seemed genuinely surprised.

"I've been to the barn on the edge of the property for different events. But no, I've never been to the house proper."

His eyes lit up. "Then you have to let me give you a tour of the place. It's still my favorite house that I've built."

"I'm sure you'd much rather enjoy the party." She followed Cole through the ornamental wood-and-glass front door.

One part of her loathed the idea of oohing and ah-hing over Duke Abbott's lavish home. Another part of her was curious to see how the other half lived.

The large entrance hall had gleaming wood floors, high ceilings and large decorative windows that let in lots of light.

He set the gifts on the entrance table and dodged two little girls who giggled as they darted through the space.

"It won't take long." Cole took the art case from her and sat it in the corner of the adjoining dining room. He headed toward the stairs. "Come on, we'll start upstairs."

Kayleigh glanced around, hoping that Parker, Savannah or someone else would appear and need her. Her curiosity had gotten the better of her. She honestly did want to tour the place, but it felt odd to traipse through their private rooms without Iris's permission.

"My parents love showing off the house," Cole assured her, as if he'd read her mind. "They won't mind— I promise."

"All right. Lead the way." Kayleigh followed him up the stairs.

Cole Abbott was the unabashed flirt of the Abbott family and a certified skirt chaser. He seemed to relish the reputation he'd earned. Kayleigh kept enough distance between them to make it clear she had no intention of being among his conquests.

The home had four bedrooms and a lovely bonus space upstairs. As they came back down the stairs, Cole was explaining how the site itself had inspired the design and materials he'd selected for the project.

"Cole. Kayleigh." Parker stood in the entrance hall, his hands balled into fists at his side.

"What's up, Park?" Cole greeted his brother cheerfully. "I was just showing Kayleigh the house. She's never been here. I was just about to show her the downstairs."

Parker's fists unfurled, but he still scowled. "Actually, Savannah sent me to find Kayleigh. We need to set up the art project for the kids," he said gruffly.

"My supplies are in the dining room." Kayleigh pointed.

"I'll grab them," Cole offered.

"No." Parker held up his large hand, palm facing his brother. "I've got it. And I'll show Kayleigh the rest of the house when we're done."

Cole frowned. "Everything okay, Park?"

"Of course." Parker relaxed his scowl and shoved his hands in his pockets.

"Since you have everything under control, I guess I'll see you guys out back." Cole turned and walked away.

"What was that about?" Kayleigh whispered loudly as she followed Parker to the dining room to retrieve her case.

"What are you talking about?" Parker shrugged innocently.

"You know *exactly* what I'm talking about. We're not on the island yet, so you can relax the whole jealous-boyfriend act."

Parker looked at her sharply, then frowned. "You don't know my brother like I do."

"Everyone in this town knows your brother's reputation." Kayleigh walked quickly to keep up with Parker's long strides. "You don't need to protect me from your brother. I've got a hell of a right hook and I can knee someone like nobody's business. Besides, he was just showing me the house."

Parker turned to look at her. He opened his mouth, then snapped it shut, as if there was something he wanted to say but couldn't. He shoved a hand in his pocket. "Sorry. I didn't mean to come off as some macho jerk."

Parker Abbott apologized?

The town should declare it Parker Abbott Apologized Day and make it an annual celebration.

"I appreciate your concern, but honestly I can take care of myself. Been doing it most of my life." She took the case from Parker. "Thank you, anyway."

Parker nodded without comment, led her to where she needed to set up for the kids and then left.

As Parker walked away, she couldn't help wondering what it was he hadn't been able to bring himself to say.

* * *

Parker sipped his bourbon-spiked sweet tea as he watched Kayleigh guide the children through a painting project. His cousin Benji's fiancée, Sloane Sutton, helped her twins, the youngest of the children.

Kayleigh was beautiful. It wasn't even summer yet, but her skin had already started to tan. The sunglasses she wore shielded her eyes, forcing him to focus on the sexy little pout of her Cupid's bow mouth. Her strong, toned arms were visible in the tank top she wore, which had an unusual cutout design at the neck and back. Tattered blue jeans offered peeks of her skin through holes at the knees and over her thighs.

Her long red hair had been in loose, shoulder-length curls when she'd arrived, but she'd swept it up in a high ponytail as she worked with the kids.

Kayleigh wiped her face with the back of her wrist, but managed to get blue paint on her face anyway. She was adorable.

This was their fifth of ten dates. Yet, rather than being happy that he was halfway through his contractual obligation, he was disappointed by how quickly their time was flying by. The realization startled him.

He'd begun to anticipate spending Saturday afternoons with Kayleigh Jemison. If he was being honest, the time he spent with Kayleigh was the highlight of his week. But maybe he was giving her too much credit. Perhaps it wasn't so much about Kayleigh as the fact that he'd spent the last weekends doing something other than working or dealing with his family.

Maybe he just needed to get a life.

"Dude. Close your mouth before something flies in it." Benji sat in the Adirondack chair beside Parker's with a beverage of his own. "At least *try* to play it cool."

Parker scowled at his cousin. "I'm watching the kids. That's the point of this party, after all."

"C'mon, Park." Benji chuckled. "You can do better than that. Or…"

Parker met his cousin's gaze, anticipating what he would say next. "Or what?"

"Or you can tell Kayleigh how you really feel about her."

Parker turned away from his cousin. He searched for another glimpse of Kayleigh before gazing out at the impressive mountain overlooking his parents' patio.

He tried to ignore his cousin's pointed stare and the feelings that had flared in his chest when he'd seen Kayleigh coming down the stairs behind Cole earlier.

It was jealousy. Plain and simple. Raw and uninhibited.

He had no claim on Kayleigh's affections or her body. She could do whatever she wanted with whomever she wanted. Still, the thought of Cole putting his hands on her had sent Parker into a brief irrational rage, even if it was only in his head.

"Ignore me, if you want, but I'm not going away." Benji poked his arm. "Neither are your feelings for her. Face it, Park, you've always had a thing for Kayleigh."

Parker narrowed his gaze at his cousin before surveying the scenery again. "You know why I'm doing this. But I just can't turn it on and off as easily as she can."

"I think you're wrong." Benji nodded toward the table where Kayleigh and the kids were. "I don't think she can, either."

When Parker glanced in her direction, his eyes met hers. She smiled, holding his gaze for a moment before returning her attention to Davis's work of art.

He swallowed hard, his heart thumping in his chest.

"See what I mean?" Benji stood, hovering over him. "Kayleigh is smart, gorgeous, adventurous… She won't stay on the market forever, Park. What happens when someone else comes along and sweeps her off her feet? You'll regret not making peace with her and telling her how you feel."

Benji walked over to the table, kissed Sloane on the cheek and then sat down to help his son Beau.

Parker heaved a sigh and finished his spiked tea. Maybe he did have feelings for Kayleigh. But that didn't mean it was in his best interest, or hers, for him to act on them. They were just too different.

Kayleigh was a free-spirited, wild child who railed against the very tenets that were the foundation of his life and the keys to his success.

They wanted very different things in life. And then there was her animosity toward his father that was bubbling just below the surface. An issue his father was well aware of, but unwilling to address.

He had absolutely no reason to believe that he and Kayleigh would make a good match. That either of them would be willing to bend enough to make a friendship, let alone a relationship, work.

His head was clear on all the reasons he shouldn't

want her, and yet…he did, with a growing desperation that made his chest ache just thinking about her, which he did often.

Parker went to the outdoor bar, where Zora had set up as the unofficial bartender.

Zora shuddered. "Looks like you could use a refill, stat."

She took his glass and filled it with sweet tea before topping it off with King's Finest bourbon and stirring. Zora handed the glass back to him.

"Want to tell me what the long face is all about, or are we just going to pretend you're not pining over a pretty little redhead?"

"Don't you start with me, too," Parker grumbled, taking a sip of his tea. "That's really strong, Zora."

"Good. You could use some mellowing out and a dose of courage," she remarked without apology.

"You let me handle my business, and I won't ask how things are between you and Dallas."

Zora's cheeks flushed at his mention of her best friend, Dallas Hamilton. "Dallas and I are just friends. Always have been. Don't try to change the subject. How is the whole dating Kayleigh thing going?"

"Fine. Better than expected, actually," he added under his breath.

Zora's eyes lit up. "Does she feel the same way?"

Parker shrugged. "We've talked about lots of things. How we feel about each other isn't one of them. Which is probably why we've been getting along so well."

"Good. I don't have to remind you how important

this deal is to all of us, or how much it's going to mean to Mom when Dad surprises her with it."

"I know what's at stake here." Parker nodded. One more reason he and Kayleigh needed to keep things strictly business between them. He was all for repairing their friendship, but anything more could derail their deal. "I won't do anything to jeopardize it. Which is why it's a bad idea to—"

"Zora, I'd love a bourbon punch, if that's possible." Kayleigh said as she joined them.

Zora glanced at him quickly before turning her attention to Kayleigh and smiling. "Pull up a seat. I just need to grab a few more lemons from inside." Zora looked at her brother pointedly. "I'll be right back."

"That looks good." Kayleigh indicated Parker's drink. "What's that?"

"Sweet tea with about a sidecar worth of bourbon." He chuckled. "Zora was a little heavy-handed for my taste."

"May I?"

He nodded, watching as she avoided his straw and sipped from the glass.

"It's good," she declared. "Strong, but good."

"Then it's yours." He put a square drink napkin in front of her and turned on the stool, his back against the bar. "The kids certainly seem to be having a good time."

"They were so adorable and their pieces all came out well. I'm going to surprise their parents and frame their pictures so they can hang them at home."

Parker couldn't find the slightest appeal in having a

piece of art created by a toddler hanging in his home, but their parents undoubtedly didn't share his view.

"I'm sure they'll appreciate it. But when will you have time to do that?"

"After we eat, they're going to put on an outdoor movie for the kids. That should give me time to frame each painting."

"The point of this whole exercise is that we spend time together." Parker straightened his shirt collar. "So I'd be happy to help."

"Thanks, Parker. That'd be great. I'll look for you after dinner." She rose from the stool, lifting her glass. "And thanks for the drink. Tell Zora thanks anyway."

"Kayleigh." He caught her hand in his and it seemed to surprise them both.

"Yes?"

He took a napkin, rubbed it against the condensation on the glass and wiped at the blue paint stain on her cheek. "You've got a little paint here."

Kayleigh thanked him, then headed back to the party, leaving her sweet scent in her wake.

Time slowed as everyone moved around Kayleigh.

Iris and Savannah cut the cake, and Sloane handed pieces out to the children. The men sat around the bar, joking with each other, and the other women sat on the patio, gossiping and catching up on each other's lives.

She'd known the Abbotts her entire life, as just about everyone in town did. But even when she and Parker had been school-age friends, their families didn't move in the same circles. In fact her family was the antithesis of the Abbotts.

They were wealthy, world-famous local royalty and beloved by all. Her family had barely skated along between utility shut-offs and vehicle repossessions. Her father's notoriety had been a perpetual stain on all of them. He'd been the most despised man in town, and everyone regarded her, her mother and her sister with a pity that clawed at her soul and burned her skin.

Leaving town hadn't solved the problem. The damage had been done. It had burrowed its way deep inside her consciousness and infected her psyche. Only once she'd moved back to Magnolia Lake had she been able to work out the demons that had haunted her. Little by little, she'd come to love the town and its people again.

Still, she hadn't extended the need for peaceful resolution to Parker Abbott or his father, Duke. She'd held onto her resentment of them like a warm blanket that warded against the cold winds of doubt that sometimes crept back in. But the past few weeks with Parker had slowly been chipping away at that protective armor.

Her close friendship with Savannah had given her occasion to get to know Blake and Zora. But she'd stayed clear of Parker and politely declined whenever her friend had invited her to functions at Duke and Iris's home.

Seeing all of the Abbotts and their extended family together this way made them seem more human. More real. The love they had for each other was evident, even in the teasing between the siblings. Duke and Iris were doting grandparents who were deeply affectionate toward their children and grandchildren.

There were so many of them. All of the Abbotts were here, including their grandfather Joseph. Sloane, Benji and their twins, along with her mother and grandfather, and his parents, sister and niece. Even Savannah's sister, Delaney, and her young daughter, Harper.

And she had…no one. Maybe she never would.

Tears burned her eyes suddenly. She'd never have her parents again, and even when they'd been in her life, their family was nothing like the Christmas-card-worthy Abbotts.

It was one more thing they had that she never would. Maybe Aidan had been her one chance at having a meaningful relationship and children of her own. Kayleigh's hand drifted to where the tears were spilling down her wet cheek. She furtively glanced around the space, hoping no one had noticed. The only thing worse than being alone in the world was being pitied because of it.

She turned around and collided with a hard body.

"We've gotta stop meeting like this, darlin'." Cole wore a good-natured grin—and his slice of cake, which she'd smashed into his pricey designer shirt.

"Cole, I'm so sorry. I ruined your shirt."

"Not one of my favorites anyway." He shrugged, licking icing from his fingers.

"I should've been paying attention. I'll get something to clean it before the stain sets."

"It's no big deal. I'll throw it in the wash and grab one

of Dad's shirts." He swiped the wetness from her cheek. "Seriously, it's nothing to cry over. It's just a shirt."

Her face stung with embarrassment and the sound of her heartbeat filled her ears.

"What did you say to her?" Parker was there suddenly, and now half of the adult eyes at the party were focused on the three of them.

"Nothing. It was an accident—that's all." Cole wiped frosting off his shirt with a napkin.

Parker looked to her as if he needed her confirmation.

"I'm sorry, Cole. I'll pay for the shirt. Excuse me."

Kayleigh wished she could disappear, or at the very least go home. But she'd promised to frame the kids' art. So she made her escape to the craft room on the lower level of the spacious home. When Kayleigh closed the door behind her, she couldn't contain the tears.

As shitty as it had been to grow up poor with only a few friends and a father who was the laughingstock of the town, it had made her strong. Impenetrable, even. Losing her father had been painful, but not unexpected, given his lifestyle. But losing her mother... that had broken her.

That had left just her and her sister. But Evvy's way of dealing with the pain was to throw herself into her new life, thousands of miles from this little town. Between school and work and the small acting jobs her sister was able to garner, they'd simply grown apart. But Kayleigh had gotten through it.

She'd met Aidan at a time when she'd felt incredibly alone. He'd been warm and supportive, and Kira had been like a sister to her. But then she'd walked away from the two of them.

The door opened and she expected Savannah, but it was Parker.

"I came bearing cake and libations." He held up a plate in one hand and her bourbon punch in the other. "Pick your poison. Or don't. You can have both."

"Thanks, Parker. Maybe later." Kayleigh swiped away the dampness on her cheeks, not meeting his gaze. "Could you just leave them?"

"Oh, sure." He put both the cake and the drink down on the work surface, away from the kids' art that Blake and Benji had transferred there earlier.

Parker opened the door to leave, but closed it again. He walked over to her. "Are you sure Cole didn't do anything…inappropriate? I saw him touch your face, and you seemed agitated."

"It wasn't because of anything Cole did. I was already upset and in tears. I was trying to leave before anyone noticed. That's how I ended up running smack-dab into Cole. Which, of course, drew everyone's attention." She sighed. "If anything, he should be angry with me for ruining his expensive shirt."

Parker stepped closer, extending a handful of napkins to her. "Then why the tears?"

She accepted the napkins, decorated with colorful balloons, the words *Happy Birthday* emblazoned on them. She wiped her cheeks, then shoved the crumpled napkins in her pocket. "You wouldn't understand."

Parker stepped closer still, his gaze trained on hers. "How do you know?"

"Because you have all of this." She gestured around them angrily, fresh tears stinging her eyes. She wiped at them, her cheeks heating with embarrassment. "And because you still have your parents, and you're surrounded by your siblings, and that's great. But you have no idea what I'm feeling right now, and I hope you never do."

He stepped closer, his voice low and his expression sincere. "I would never have invited you here if I'd realized how it would impact you."

"It isn't your fault." She sniffled. "And I'm not normally like this. I can't remember the last time I cried about anything. Besides, I'd already promised Savannah that I'd come to the party before they decided to have it here. I couldn't miss Davis's birthday."

Parker's eyes were filled with what seemed like genuine compassion, as awkward silence stretched between them. He stepped close enough that his enticing scent tickled her nostrils and his heat enveloped her. His dark eyes locked with hers as he took another step forward.

He slowly lifted his hands and cradled her jaw as he lowered his head, closing the space between them.

Kayleigh squeezed her eyes shut, her heart beating faster.

His lips met hers in a kiss that was tender and sweet. Yet her body burned for him as she leaned into his touch, her hands pressed to his firm chest.

She knew that he'd kissed her out of a sense of pity. She didn't want Parker's pity, but she did want this. His firm, sensual lips on hers. His strong hands gently cradling her face. His hard body braced against hers.

He tilted her head back, and she parted her lips in response. A soft murmur rose in her throat when his tongue swept between her lips.

Warmth filled her chest, and her belly fluttered as he deepened their kiss. His mouth tasted rich and sweet. Like bourbon, sweet tea and buttercream frosting.

Parker's hands dropped to her waist and she gasped when he lifted her onto the table, without breaking their kiss.

His hands found her lower back as he pulled her closer to the table's edge. The ridge beneath his zipper pressed against the growing heat between her thighs, making her want things with Parker Abbott that she shouldn't.

Her pulse raced as Parker's large hands slipped beneath her shirt, his fingertips skimming her back.

She wrapped her arms around his neck, pulling him closer, desperate for more of the unexpected connection between them.

The door opened suddenly, startling both of them. They turned toward the sound.

"I'm sorry, I didn't mean to… I just wanted to make sure Kayleigh was all right," Savannah stammered. "I'll just go. Let me know if you need anything."

Her friend was gone before either of them could respond.

Kayleigh's face stung with heat and her heart raced. She didn't meet Parker's gaze as she slid off the table and out of his reach. She folded her arms over her chest, shielding the evidence of her body's intense reaction to his.

"We should get the framing done." She moved toward the back of the room, where the frames were lined up.

Parker ran a hand over his head and sighed. "I know I shouldn't have done that, but—"

"Let's just consider it practice. You know…in case the situation arises while we're at Kira's wedding." She tested the paint on the children's artwork to see if it was dry without looking up at him.

"I'm sorry about your parents and about you and Evvy." His voice was warm and reassuring. "If there's anything I can do—"

"Thank you, but I'm fine now." She glanced up briefly before returning her attention to the paintings. "Now, if we work together, we can get all of these framed in no time."

"Just tell me what you need."

What she needed was…him. The comfort of his embrace. The warmth of his kiss. To not feel alone.

She asked him to hand her one of the frames instead and tried desperately to convince herself that she didn't want Parker to kiss her again.

Eight

Kayleigh sat across the booth from Savannah at Magnolia Lake Bakery after yoga, sipping her mocha latte.

Savannah still looked stunned, despite the fact that they'd broken down the kiss between her and Parker, as well as everything that had led up to it.

Who could blame her? Kayleigh had had two days to digest and rehash the events and she was still just as surprised.

"Does that mean Project Friendship has now become Project Relationship?" Savannah sipped her peach-mango smoothie.

"As far as I can tell, neither of us is looking for a relationship. I'm not even sure we'll come out of this as friends exactly." Kayleigh shrugged. "But I do know that, for the sake of the deal, we both need to remain focused on our objectives."

Kayleigh sipped her mocha latte and returned the oversize cup to the table. "Getting through Kira's wedding without incident is my only concern, and it should be his, too. The deal hinges upon it. Anything else is an unnecessary complication neither of us can afford."

"Believe me, I understand where you're coming from. This is supposed to be about what your head wants, not your heart." Savannah sighed. "But I also understand how quickly a plan like this can go off the rails when you're battling your emotions and physical attraction. It isn't easy to ignore feelings like that, whether it's love or desire."

"Whoa, no one said anything about the *L* word." Kayleigh held up a hand.

"So maybe love isn't an issue…yet." Savannah looked at her pointedly, one brow raised. "But from what I saw, the other *L* word, *lust*, was definitely in play. Who knows how far you two would've taken things if I hadn't interrupted you."

Kayleigh's cheeks burned, the possibilities flashing in her brain. "Things wouldn't have gone that far. Not there," she added.

"But you and Parker have that camping trip coming up this weekend. He's just spending one night at the site, right?" Savannah pulled off a piece of her warm sticky bun and practically purred when she put it in her mouth.

"Actually, there's been a change of plans and a compromise." Kayleigh had hoped the topic wouldn't come up.

"What kind of change?"

"I've agreed to accompany him to New York for the weekend when he attends one of his industry events in a couple of weeks, so he thought it would only be fair if he stayed the full weekend when we go camping."

"Right. That's the week our whole family will be in the Bahamas." Savannah nodded, then hiked an eyebrow as she leaned back, arms folded. "Wait… Parker *volunteered* to spend an entire weekend at a campground site with public bathrooms and an outdoor shower? That's surprisingly charitable of him. What's the compromise?"

"That we *don't* spend the weekend at a campground site with a public bathroom and an outdoor shower." Kayleigh sipped her latte slowly, allowing the large cup to shield much of her face.

"I thought you were a purist when it comes to camping." Savannah could barely hold back her smirk.

"I am when I'm paying for it," she muttered. "Parker insisted on the upgrade, so he's paying the difference."

"And what about when you two go to New York?"

"Separate rooms, of course." Kayleigh didn't meet her friend's gaze, didn't want to see the questions and implications there. "And King's Finest is paying for my flight and hotel since I'm accompanying him to an industry event."

"Just be honest with yourself and each other about how you feel. I know Parker comes off as this curmudgeonly turtle with a hard shell who only peeks his head and limbs out when it's absolutely necessary, but he's more vulnerable than he believes he is, especially when it comes to you. What happened Saturday proves that he's a lot more into you than either of you might realize."

"I never asked Parker to run interference between me and Cole. Nor did I ask him to kiss me."

"And yet he did." Savannah nibbled another bite of her sticky bun. "He's already in way over his head, but he still thinks he's standing safely on the shore."

"You've got a soft spot for Parker." Kayleigh cut her muffin in half. "Even after he tried to toss you in jail?"

"To be fair, he thought I was a corporate spy trying to steal proprietary information to sell to their competitors," Savannah said, her tone serious. "So I can't much blame him for being angry at the time. Or for his initial objections to his grandfather giving my family what was rightfully owed to us. But that was three years ago. Our relationship has come a long way since then."

"You've been charmed by Oscar the Grouch." Kayleigh teased.

"Well, you kissed him, so I'm pretty sure I'm the one who's winning." Savannah giggled, drinking the last of her smoothie.

"Good point." Kayleigh laughed. "I'll admit, I'm seeing Parker in a new light the more time we spend together. I'll keep what you've said in mind. I promise."

"That's all I ask." Savannah smiled sadly. "You're both family to me. I don't want to see either of you get hurt."

Kayleigh's heart swelled. Savannah, having lost her parents at a young age in a fire, understood Kayleigh's pain and loss. Perhaps even more deeply. So saying that she considered them to be family… Savannah understood just how much that meant to Kayleigh. That it made her feel a little less alone in the world.

Nine

Kayleigh stood in Parker's driveway with Cricket by her side as he loaded his duffel bags into the back of the Jeep. The golden retriever still wasn't a fan of Parker's, mostly because he usually ignored her, but at least she wasn't growling and baring her teeth at him.

So…progress.

Since they wouldn't be needing the tents, sleeping bags, heater or propane stove, there was plenty of room for his oversize bags.

"You do realize we're only staying for the weekend and formal attire isn't required?" Kayleigh teased as he loaded the last of his things into the back.

"In the event of a zombie apocalypse, I've got you covered," he said, nearly straight-faced.

"Can't argue with that logic." She laughed.

Parker had just referenced her favorite television show and he wasn't taking himself too seriously. Also progress. Maybe their weekend together wouldn't be so bad.

"Hey, Cricket, how are you this morning, girl?" Parker waved at her, smiling.

Cricket turned to Kayleigh, seemingly as surprised by Parker's direct address as she was.

Kayleigh patted the dog's back to ensure her that the zombie apocalypse hadn't arrived and left them with a zombified version of Parker Abbott.

Cricket walked over and sniffed the part of Parker's leg left bare by his navy cargo shorts. When Cricket seemed satisfied, she looked up at Parker.

Kayleigh laughed. "It seems you passed the sniff test. I believe she's waiting for you to pet her."

Parker patted the dog's side twice. "Good girl. Ready for our weekend adventure?"

Cricket barked, then jumped into the back seat when Kayleigh opened the door for her.

"Guess that means she is." Kayleigh closed the door behind her and opened the driver's door. She stared at Parker, who'd already gotten in on the passenger side. "I was up late finishing a few orders before our trip. Interested in driving?"

"You'd trust me to drive the Cricketmobile?" He straightened his glasses.

"We both know that, of the two of us, you're the safer driver." Kayleigh tossed Parker the keys and they traded places. She strapped on her seat belt.

Parker got into the driver's seat. He reviewed the

location of the turn signals, windshield wipers and hazard lights. Then he asked about the brakes and inquired about when the oil was last changed. Kayleigh was starting to regret her decision to let Parker drive, but then he finally pulled onto the road.

They'd been driving in silence for a bit when Kayleigh summoned the nerve to broach the topic they were both avoiding.

"So, about that day at your parents' place…" It was a lame but effective opening line. "That was weird, right?"

Parker tightened his grip on the steering wheel and his expression tensed, but he didn't take his eyes off the road.

"It's weird that a guy would want to kiss you?"

"It's weird that *you'd* want to kiss me. It's not like you're my biggest fan." She studied his expression, hating that she could only see half of it.

"I'm not the one who declared war, Kayleigh." There was a sadness in his tone that stabbed at her chest. "But to your point, it wasn't something I set out deliberately to do. It just sort of…happened."

"That's why I thought we should talk about it before we spend the next two weekends together." Kayleigh tried to keep her tone upbeat. "Because I think it's best if we don't have any misunderstandings."

"Like?"

"Like I don't want you to think that this is some convoluted scheme designed to—"

"Get me into bed?" Parker smiled slyly.

"Or into a relationship," she added.

He frowned. "If I offended you, I'm sorry."

"You didn't offend me, Parker." She touched his arm. It seemed to startle him, so she withdrew her hand. "And I obviously reciprocated. I guess what I'm saying is… we shouldn't get caught up in the moment, because this is just a temporary arrangement."

"I agree." Parker nodded. "I'm not a person who acts on emotion, and I didn't intend to kiss you. I just…" He glanced at her quickly before returning his attention to the road. "You were incredibly sad. I just wanted to console you. Honestly, I'm not sure what I was thinking. Guess I wasn't. But I'm glad we can move past it. I know you're going to like this cabin. The view is amazing, and it's quiet and secluded."

Kayleigh was grateful Parker had shifted the conversation back to safe ground and that they'd come to an understanding. Now that they'd gotten that practice kiss out of the way, they just needed to follow the same rules they'd learned in kindergarten: keep your hands and lips to yourselves.

Then everything would be just fine.

Parker readjusted his pillow and checked his watch. It was well after midnight, and though he'd turned in for the night two hours earlier, sleep had yet to find him.

He threw an arm across his face, shielding it from the sliver of moonlight visible through a gap in the curtains.

The logical option was to get up and pull them closed, but his weary, aching muscles refused to comply.

Despite Kayleigh's claims of being tired, she and

Cricket possessed a boundless well of energy he simply didn't. For the first full day of their trip, Kayleigh had insisted on hiking the area, taking photographs of foliage, wildlife and the landscape. She collected interesting rocks and pieces of wood for future projects.

She hadn't compelled him to go. In fact she'd suggested the hike might be too much for him. Which, of course, made him more determined to show her that he wasn't the lethargic desk-sitter she imagined him to be.

The only problem with his plan was that he was indeed a lethargic desk-sitter. His work in his home gym had toned and carved his muscles, but his aversion to cardio and sweating revealed itself in their fourth or fifth mile of hiking.

He'd nearly fallen face-first into his plate during their late dinner, excusing himself afterward for a long soak in the tub.

But after a couple of hours of fitful sleep, he was awake again. Visions of Kayleigh danced in his head. He'd spent hours trudging behind her as she hiked in those enticing khaki shorts that accentuated the shapely curve of her perfect bottom. The length of the shorts made her legs appear to go on for miles, despite the muddy, worn hiking boots she wore.

The racerback athletic shirt highlighted the long, lean column of her graceful neck and the muscles of her back. Her curly red hair swung in a ponytail that peeked through the back of the khaki baseball hat pulled down low over her eyes. And her thighs...

Parker sat up abruptly against the headboard. He

pressed the heels of his hands to his tired eyes and heaved a sigh.

Kayleigh had been clear that, from her perspective, nothing had changed regarding the temporary nature of their arrangement. This was all simply research for the roles they would play in just a few weeks. Then things would go back to the way they were. Reliving his spectacular view of Kayleigh's curves during their afternoon hike was counterproductive to that objective.

He threw off the sheets, pulled on a T-shirt, and stalked across the hardwood floor and down to the kitchen for a warm glass of milk.

When he entered the kitchen, half of the large deck, visible through the kitchen window overlooking the mountains, was lit. The lights were on in the room that housed the indoor swimming pool.

Parker followed the sound of water splashing.

"Kayleigh?" He stood beside the heated, indoor pool. "I can't believe you're still up. I would've expected you two to crash after the day we had."

"One of us did." She pointed to Cricket, who was lying in the corner, sleeping peacefully. "But I couldn't sleep."

She went back to swimming laps in the pool. Her lean, strong arms effortlessly sliced through the water; she had a beautiful freestyle. When she reached the wall, she went directly into a backstroke.

Parker stood beside the pool, mesmerized. There was something simply entrancing about the movement of her body whether she was in the water, on foot or on a bicycle.

Kayleigh finished the last of her laps and climbed the stairs out of the pool, giving him a full view of her red halter bikini.

She looked…incredible. Narrow waist, toned abs, strong arms and lean, muscular thighs that he kept envisioning wrapped around his waist.

"Parker." She'd said his name as if she'd called it more than once to get his attention. "Would you hand me a towel, please?"

She removed the band that kept her hair up in a topknot and wrung the excess water from it.

"Thanks." Kayleigh wrapped the towel around her loosely, tucking it beneath her arm to secure it. She put her hair back in a much looser topknot before nodding toward the hot tub in the far corner. "I'm getting into the hot tub. You should join me. I worked you pretty hard today, but you were a trouper."

He swallowed hard. *Mind out of the gutter, Park. Mind out of the gutter.*

"I'm not wearing my trunks, but I'll keep you company."

"I thought you went to bed hours ago. Did I wake you?" She wrapped her damp hair in a second towel.

"Couldn't sleep. I came downstairs for a warm glass of milk."

"I couldn't sleep either." She bit her lower lip and glanced away momentarily. "I think I'm too wound up after today. And this place is amazing. I've never stayed in a cabin this nice. I still can't believe it has an indoor pool, a game room and this amazing view."

Kayleigh stepped closer to the wall of glass windows

facing the mountains. She turned to him suddenly. "I've got just the thing to knock you out. I'll be right back."

He should go to bed. Leave her to her hot tub while he got some sleep and tried not to think of her in that bikini. But he stayed rooted in place, because the truth was that he was eager to spend more time with her. Even if that meant keeping her company while she soaked in the hot tub in the wee hours of the morning.

Kayleigh returned, her flip-flops slapping against the stone floor. She held a jug he recognized as one of the moonshines they'd released to commemorate the King's Finest Jubilee three years earlier.

"You held onto that bottle all this time?" He grabbed two of the stemless silicone wine glasses stored behind the poolside bar.

"Savannah gave it to me one year on my birthday. I'd been saving it for…" Her cheeks suddenly turned pink. "I thought I'd bring it along to thank you for the upgrade. I might have been wrong about this whole glamping thing. Camping in luxury isn't so bad."

She handed him the jug, kicked her flip-flops off and slid into the warm water of the hot tub. Parker opened the bottle, poured a little in each of their glasses and handed her one.

"You know, drinking makes you sleepy, but it doesn't actually help you sleep better. It's been proven to inter-fere with sleep patterns." He dragged one of the heavy chairs closer to the hot tub and sank onto it.

"Humor me." She sipped her drink. "Mmm… Savan-nah was right. The peach cobbler is amazing."

"It's my favorite, too." He inhaled the luscious peach

aroma before tipping the glass and allowing the slow burn to spread through his body. "But drinking it always makes me feel like a cliché. A rural Southern person camping in the mountains and drinking moonshine. How original."

"Don't be so high-and-mighty, Abbott. Your family wouldn't be sitting on that wad of cash now if it wasn't for the moonshine operation your great-grandfather ran in these very mountains back in the day."

"True." He sipped from his glass. If it weren't for King Abbott's moonshine operation, his grandfather Joseph Abbott would never have started a legitimate distillery. Parker set his glass down on a nearby table. There was something else he'd much rather talk about. "Kayleigh, can I ask you something?"

"You can ask." She set her glass down, too. "But I reserve the right not to answer."

"Fair enough." He scooted toward the edge of the seat. "This Aidan guy and his sister...you said they were important to you."

"They were." She frowned. "We covered this already. Do I need to call Cricket over?"

"Cricket is sleeping," he reminded her.

Kayleigh groaned, taking another sip from her glass. "Okay, so what is it that you so desperately need to know about my relationship with Aidan?"

"If you loved him so much, why didn't you fight for your relationship, or at the very least tell him what his mother did and let him decide?"

She narrowed her gaze and pursed her lips. "It was a no-win proposition. If he chose me, then there would always be tension between his mother and us. If he chose her…" Her words faded and she emptied her glass before returning it to the ledge and sinking deeper into the warm water.

"You were afraid that if you gave him a choice, he wouldn't choose you." Parker spoke softly, saying the words more to himself than to her.

Kayleigh climbed out of the hot tub, slipped on her flip-flops and wrapped the towel around her again. "It's late, and I'm suddenly very tired. I'll see you at breakfast."

"Kayleigh." Parker gripped her hand. "I didn't mean to upset you."

"Then why do you keep asking about my relationship with Aidan when you know I don't want to talk about it?"

"Because I'm trying to understand."

"Trying to understand what?" Her shoulders tensed.

"You're a fighter. You always have been. So I'm just trying to understand why you won't fight to save your relationships with the people you care about."

Kayleigh snatched her hand from his. "A few dates and suddenly you think you've got my entire life figured out? Well, you don't, Abbott. You don't know anything about who I am or what I'm willing to fight for."

"I know you were willing to dig your heels in and fight me and my father—even when it wasn't to your advantage. Yet you weren't willing to fight for your relationship with Aidan, Kira or Evvy…or your friendship with me."

Kayleigh's eyes widened and her brows furrowed.

The color seemed to drain from her cheeks. Her chest hitched as she shook her head. "I should never have asked you to do this."

She turned and hurried away from him, her wet flip-flops slapping against the stone.

Parker jumped to his feet to go after her, but Cricket, who was up and on Kayleigh's heels, barked at him, then growled before following her mistress out of the room.

Don't be a jackass, Parker.

He had one rule to follow. Yet he couldn't seem to manage it. Kayleigh didn't want to talk about Aidan or Evvy. She'd been crystal clear about that. But he hadn't been able to help himself. He was compelled to understand her and why she'd written off their friendship without even allowing him to explain.

Parker dropped back onto the chair, wishing he'd stayed in bed and kept his big mouth shut.

Ten

Kayleigh pushed herself, running as fast as she could for the final mile back to the cabin. The cool, brisk early morning breeze was a relief against her heated skin, damp with perspiration.

She'd gotten up before the sun rose and hit the mountain trail as soon as there was enough light, hoping to avoid Parker.

Fucking Parker Abbott.

Once a jerk, always a jerk.

Aside from the still inexplicable kiss, things had been going pretty well between them. They were getting along, even enjoying each other's company. And Cricket was just beginning to come around to Parker. But deep down he was still that persistent little boy who would pick at a sore, pulling off the scab and wrecking the healing process.

She understood why Parker had some curiosity about the Brennans. After all, he was attending Kira's wedding and had been roped into an elaborate scheme for their benefit. So she'd allowed for his first round of questions about her relationship with the family and tolerated the second. But, as always, Parker Abbott just didn't recognize when she was at her limit. And the guy was still terrible at taking a hint. Even when she'd spelled it out for him pretty plainly.

She'd been so angry, she'd wanted to take Cricket and hop into her truck in her wet swimming suit and drive back to Magnolia Lake, leaving Abbott to fend for himself.

Maybe he would've gotten the hint then.

Kayleigh gasped with relief when the cabin finally came into view. Her muscles ached and sweat dripped into her eyes. Her feet hurt and she had calluses. And she was thirsty enough to drink from a trough.

But at least she'd given herself some distance from Parker. Some time to decide what she should do next. She hadn't been perceptive enough to add a Parker's-a-total-jerk clause to the contract.

Would she be able to pull out of the contract, even if Parker hadn't violated it in any way?

Kayleigh collapsed on the front steps of the large porch, her chest heaving as she tried to catch her breath.

Her head was pounding, her body ached, and she and

Cricket needed water. But she honestly wasn't sure she could move another muscle.

The front door creaked opened, but she didn't turn around. She hoped Parker would get the hint and go away. When the door clicked shut without a word, she squeezed her eyes closed and released a long breath. Partly in relief, partly in disappointment.

"I know you're thirsty, girl." Kayleigh rubbed Cricket's soft fur, then patted her side as the dog panted. "Give Mama a moment to catch her breath."

A few seconds later, the door creaked open again. This time the sound was followed by Parker's footsteps as he descended the stairs and placed a bowl filled with water on the ground for Cricket. He sat on the step above Kayleigh and extended a cold bottle of water to her without saying a word.

Kayleigh raised her eyes to his and sighed.

She wanted so badly to tell Parker Abbott exactly what he could do with that bottle of water, but she was desperate for hydration.

"Thank you," she muttered, lowering her gaze to the bottle as she accepted it. She unscrewed the cap and drank until the bottle was empty.

Parker took the empty bottle from her hand and screwed the top back on it before leaning back on his elbows. "How far'd you run?"

She checked her fitness watch. "Six and a half miles."

"Without water?" He turned to her and frowned.

"I had water for both of us. I just didn't expect to run so far." She readjusted the baseball cap on her head and wiped the perspiration from her eyes with the back of her wrist.

"You were that angry with me, huh?" He held her gaze.

Kayleigh stood quickly, prepared to make her escape, but her right calf cramped.

She sat back down on the step and rubbed the pained muscle.

"May I?" Parker set the bottle aside and indicated her leg, his large hands hovering just above it.

Kayleigh sighed, nodding. Her cheeks stung with heat. She couldn't even pull off a decent dramatic exit.

Parker turned toward her and gently placed his hands on her leg, extending her calf.

"Pull the toes toward your knee. That'll help relieve the cramp."

Parker supported the weight of her leg as she did the extensions repeatedly.

"That's good. Now just relax your leg." He rested her leg across his own, his strong hands massaging her calf.

His hands moved deftly, alleviating the pain and causing warmth to spread along her skin, culminating in the space between her thighs.

She was suddenly conscious of her hardened nipples, accentuated by the rapid rise and fall of her chest.

"Thank you." She halted his motion and withdrew her leg. She was able to stand easily, but some of the pain lingered.

"It feels much better. I'm going to hop into a nice, hot shower."

"Actually, you should ice it first." Parker said. "When the pain has diminished, then you can take your hot shower."

"Thanks." Kayleigh put weight on her right leg as she climbed the next step, but she winced in pain.

"I've got you." Parker stood, sweeping her up in his arms before she could object.

She gasped in surprise, her hand pressed against his strong chest as he carried her up the remaining stairs and into the cabin.

Kayleigh wanted to insist that he put her down. She was hot, sticky, sweaty and smelled like the great outdoors. Parker was a germophobe. She could only imagine how grossed out he must be. But he didn't flinch or complain as he took her inside, then carried her up to her bedroom on the second floor and set her down on the edge of the large soaking tub.

"Sit tight. I'll get some ice." He returned with a plastic bag full of ice, wrapped it in a towel and handed it to her. "Let me know if you need anything else. I'm going to order us some breakfast. Eggs, waffles, bacon, sausage and orange juice?"

"That'd be great." Kayleigh positioned the ice over her calf. "Thank you, Parker."

He nodded and left the room while Cricket lay down at her feet on the cool terra-cotta bathroom tile.

She didn't understand Parker, and maybe she never would.

One moment he'd accused her of being a coward who was too afraid to fight for the people she loved. The next he was caring for her and Cricket as if he…

No, she would not give him credit for imitating a decent human being. Parker was all about business. His actions were sweet and thoughtful on the surface, and she appreciated what he'd done. But this was all about the deal for Parker. He'd done what he felt he needed to do to ensure that their deal was still on.

Kayleigh set the ice in the sink and turned on the shower, reminding herself to never forget that.

Eleven

Parker carefully unpacked their breakfast and laid it out on the table on the back deck overlooking the mountains and lush green forest. He glanced up as Kayleigh approached.

A short, flared white skirt showed off her strong, feminine legs, while a black off-shoulder blouse accentuated her toned shoulders and graceful neck. Her hair, still wet from the shower, appeared much darker and hung in perfect ringlets.

"This looks and smells amazing." She surveyed the spread and sat in the seat he'd indicated. She waited until they were both settled at the table before she took her first bite and groaned with pleasure.

The sensual sound vibrated through his chest and

settled below his belt. He gulped some of the freshly squeezed orange juice.

"So, about last night," Parker said after they'd enjoyed most of their meal in relative silence.

Kayleigh frowned and sipped her juice. "Maybe it's better if we forget about last night."

Parker hesitated for a moment, but then put his fork down and scanned her pained expression.

"I didn't intend to make you angry."

"I believe you, Parker." Kayleigh nibbled on her last piece of bacon. "I guess I got so angry because…" She shrugged. "Maybe there's some truth to what you said."

Kayleigh was conceding to his observation?

He was speechless.

"So this awards event next weekend in New York…" Kayleigh finally said after another stretch of silence. "I assume I should dress up for it."

"If you'd like." He shrugged. "I'm only staying at the gala long enough to collect the award."

"For?"

"Distillery executive of the year." He drank the last of his juice.

"That's quite an honor. You're just going to accept the prize and bounce? Seems rude." Her tone made it sound more like an observation than an accusation. And she was probably right.

"I don't care much for large social events. I spend the entire evening checking my watch and calculating the appropriate time to make my escape." Parker chugged the last of his orange juice.

"What's your biggest fear about attending them?" Kayleigh's dark brown eyes assessed his.

"Other than the fact that I don't enjoy spending my evenings making inconsequential talk with strangers?"

"It's an industry event. You must be acquainted with some of your competitors and vendors."

"I am." He rubbed the back of his neck. "But that usually means enduring long, painful conversations. A vendor once cornered me and showed me photos of all twenty of his grandchildren."

"You're a real charmer, aren't you?" Kayleigh rolled her eyes and sighed. "It's called building relationships, Abbott. You get to know them. You allow them to get to know you. Then they're more inclined to purchase from your company in the future. It's a little thing we like to call networking, and it's an essential part of every business."

"Fortunately Max, Zora, Blake and my dad excel at it."

"But they won't be there next weekend. You will. Who knows what type of connection you might make, if you're willing to make the effort."

"You sound like Zora." Parker groaned.

"It's no different than what you've been doing with me the past few weeks. Asking questions about my life. At least feigning interest—"

"I *am* genuinely concerned about your life and about what you've been through," he said abruptly. Was he that much of a bastard that even now she still didn't believe he was genuinely interested in her?

"I appreciate the effort," she said. "And I'm sure

that the people you'll encounter at the event next week would, too."

"Point taken, but there's one more thing…" Parker frowned, remembering the awkward dance he and Kayleigh had shared at Blake and Savannah's wedding reception. "You already know I'm not much of a dancer. If I hang around too long at these things, someone inevitably asks me to dance. I either hurt their feelings by turning them down or make a fool of myself by attempting to accommodate them. Neither situation is ideal."

"That was a painful experience," Kayleigh groused. She shook her head at the memory. "But you don't need to be Usher or Fred Astaire. A little hip swaying should get you through the night just fine. All you need is a couple of moves and a little bit of swagger."

"I'm pretty sure I don't have either. When it comes to dancing," he clarified.

"You can learn them." Kayleigh stood, gathering their plates. She paused and glanced over at him. "How long before we need to check out of the cabin?"

"I booked it for tonight, too. Just in case you wanted to stay until later this evening. We could even leave first thing tomorrow morning, if you'd like."

She froze, pinning him with an incredulous stare before returning her attention to gathering the plates. "That was very generous of you, Parker."

He stood and collected the remaining food, then followed her to the kitchen.

"Give me a few minutes to load the dishwasher. Then meet me beside the pool for your dance lesson."

"I appreciate the offer, but I'm sure you'd rather spend your last few hours here relaxing and enjoying the view."

"I'm not going to let you accept that award and dash out next week. And if I'm getting all dressed up, we're staying and dancing," she replied. "So I'm doing this for my own safety."

He'd stepped on her foot inadvertently and they'd nearly stumbled during their last dance together.

"Fair enough. What time would you like to check out?" He asked the question nonchalantly, hoping it wasn't too obvious that he wanted to spend another evening with her. This time he'd keep his observations about Kayleigh's life to himself.

"Why don't we play it by ear?"

Parker's jaw clenched involuntarily. He was practically allergic to spontaneity, a fact Kayleigh was well aware of. She seemed hell-bent on bashing in every single wall of his carefully constructed comfort zone with a steel battering ram. But he would do his best to adapt.

He nodded. "Sure. Why not?"

Kayleigh seemed stunned that he'd agreed so easily. She nabbed one last piece of bacon before he shut the lid on the container. "See you on the dance floor in five."

Twelve

Parker stared at his feet and repeated the line dance steps in his head. Patterns he understood, so he could easily remember what he was *supposed* to be doing. But once he tried to move in sync with the music, everything fell apart.

"It's pointless." He stopped his painfully uncoordinated movements and ran a hand over his head. "Dancing isn't my gift. I've made peace with it."

Kayleigh paused the song on her cell phone. "You know the steps. Just stop thinking so much and connect with the music."

"I'm trying to move with the beat."

"And it looks painful." Her warm tone and sweet smile took the sting out of her words. "So let's try something less structured."

"What do you have in mind?" He was grateful for the reprieve.

"A basic step, touch." She demonstrated the move.

He watched her do it a few times, then moved in sync with her. "This is easy enough. Why didn't we start with this?"

"It's too early to get cocky, Abbott." She stopped dancing and faced him, indicating that he continue as she assessed him. "Soften your knees and take smaller steps. Don't stomp your foot. You're not killing bugs. Just tap your toes lightly. You'll be lighter on your feet and you can easily shift your weight in preparation for the next step."

He felt awkward dancing while Kayleigh critiqued him. But he tried diligently to incorporate each new instruction.

"Much better." She switched to a mellow love ballad. Her brown eyes twinkled and one side of her mouth quirked. "My big toe may never forgive me for this, but why don't we take another stab at dancing together?"

Parker placed one hand near the top of her back and gripped her hand with the other, holding it high. He could still remember his grade school phys ed instructor barking at them to hold the frame.

"We're not doing the waltz, so this position feels too formal. Loosen up a little. Also, I won't bite, so you don't need to leave enough space between us to set up a lemonade stand."

"Loosen the hold and hold the lemonade stand. Got it." He catalogued her instructions in his brain. Parker stepped closer, glided his palm down her back a little and lowered their clasped hands. "Like this?"

"Much better." Kayleigh pressed her hand to his back. "Let's go back into that step, touch move."

They practiced to one song, then another, until he felt more confident.

"Better, but you're still a little stiff. You realize your hips are capable of movement, right?"

"Obviously." He smirked.

"Not *that* kind of hip movement." Kayleigh's cheeks flushed. "Maybe we should practice hip circles."

"That's a definite no for me." He came to a stop and released her. "But if you'd care to practice hip circles, I'm happy to critique you."

"That's a great idea. But don't just assess them— practice them with me." She huffed in response to his adamant refusal. "Okay, you don't have to. Just try to *feel* the music."

"I'll try to do a better job of keeping time with the music. How's that?"

"Close enough." Kayleigh scrolled through her phone. The opening chords of Marvin Gaye's "Got to Give It Up" played and she set it down. "This is perfect. It's up-tempo with a really funky, sexy groove."

Strung together, those words didn't make sense to him. "What exactly am I supposed to be doing?"

"Same as before." She started the step, touch again. "Just remember, you're not a utility pole, so your hips and waist shouldn't be stationary."

Parker followed her lead and tried to be more relaxed, like Kayleigh. Arms raised and hips rocking, she snapped her fingers and sang along. He was mesmerized.

He concentrated on the music and Kayleigh's movements—smooth, hypnotic and sexy as hell. Little by little, each move felt more natural.

"All right now!" Kayleigh grinned, her body swaying. She turned, giving her back to him as she swiveled her hips.

She was close. Close enough for her signature vanilla scent to tickle his nostrils. Close enough for him to feel the heat radiating from her freshly scrubbed skin. But not close enough to touch.

Yet that's exactly what he wanted. To wrap his arms around her waist and haul her body against his as they danced together.

"Awesome job, Parker." She high-fived him when the song ended. "Now we'll do the same thing back in partner position to a slower song."

"Got it." He mentally reviewed everything he'd learned as she selected the next song. Another Marvin Gaye tune: "I Want You."

Apropos choice.

He took her in his arms and they swayed to the song, which she played on repeat.

"You're doing terrific, Parker." The encouragement in her voice warmed his chest and made him want to try harder.

Next she showed him how to use the gentle pressure of both hands to guide her as they made their way across the floor.

"You're actually going to let me lead?" he teased.

"Don't let it go to your head, and don't make us look bad." Her body fit snugly against his as she pressed her cheek to his chest.

It was a welcome sensation.

Parker cradled her soft curves against him and rested his chin against the top of her head, inhaling the sweet scent of her shampoo.

"So, what's the verdict?" he asked. "Am I ready for prime time?"

"Definitely." Kayleigh looked up at him. There was something in her tone and expression he couldn't quite read. She pulled out of his embrace and turned off the music. "That's enough practice. I'll go pack so we can get out of here."

"Kayleigh." Parker caught her hand when she turned to walk away. "Was it something I said?"

"No." She shook her head, not meeting his gaze. "It's nothing like that."

"But it is *something*." Parker stepped closer.

Kayleigh bit her lower lip. Her chest rose and fell quickly, as if she was in distress.

"Talk to me, Kayleigh." He needed to see the depths of those brown eyes to make sure he hadn't sabotaged the progress they'd made. He gently lifted Kayleigh's chin, and her gaze met his. "Why are you suddenly so agitated?"

"It's nothing. I…" She sighed heavily as she slipped her hand from his. But rather than pulling away, she clutched his shirt with both hands and lifted onto her toes. Her eyes drifted shut as she pressed her lips to his.

* * *

Kayleigh Jemison was sure she'd lost her freaking mind. She was kissing Parker Abbott. *Intentionally.*

Parker seemed stunned at first. He'd gone still, allowing her to take control. But then his strong hands drifted to the back of her neck. His thumbs rested against her cheekbones as he kissed her.

The kiss started off tame and sweet as they felt each other out. But their tentativeness slowly gave way to the heat growing between them. He sucked on her lower lip before tilting her head, sliding his warm tongue inside her mouth and gliding it against hers.

She welcomed it with an involuntary sigh.

Parker was an excellent kisser. She could add that to the long list of things about him that surprised her.

He'd been utterly adorable as he'd struggled to learn to dance. But as they danced to a slow song together, in full contact, hips in motion, his lean, fit body pressed to hers, she couldn't help wanting him to kiss her again. Something she'd fantasized about since he'd kissed her at his parents' house.

The memory of that first kiss often flooded her brain, the sensations washing over her with the same intensity they had that day. Each time, she dismissed the prospect of repeating their mistake.

It was a colossally bad idea that would only complicate their arrangement. Yet she couldn't help wanting him.

She wanted to feel his strong hands on her bare skin, and to run her fingertips along his. She wanted to trace the muscles of his calves and biceps, which she'd ogled shamelessly during their hike through the mountains. And she desperately needed to know if his abs and ass were as firm as their perfect outlines, visible through his clothing, led her to believe.

Her pulse raced and her temperature rose in response to his deepening of their kiss. A spark of electricity danced along her spine as he trailed one large hand down her back. Her nipples pebbled as they brushed against his firm chest.

As delicious as his kiss was, it only made her want more than was possible with the two of them still fully dressed. Kayleigh fumbled with the buttons on Parker's shirt. She'd unfastened two when he pulled his mouth from hers suddenly.

He seemed thrown off by her taking control again. He studied her, his chest heaving. But he didn't speak. Nor did he halt her progress as she unbuttoned the remaining buttons.

She slipped the fabric from his shoulders. His hungry gaze locked with hers as he allowed the shirt to fall to the floor.

Kayleigh sank her teeth into her lower lip and sighed softly as she studied his lean, muscular frame.

Parker certainly hadn't earned those pecs and biceps from sitting at his desk all day, crunching numbers.

His hands dropped to her waist, then drifted up her rib cage as he lifted the hem of her blouse and tugged it over her head.

Her chest rose and fell heavily and her belly tightened beneath his gaze as he studied the sheer black bralette that did little to hide how aroused she was by him. Parker glided the backs of his fingers up her stomach, then teased one of the pebbled nubs with his thumb.

He grazed the hardened peak with his teeth through the lacy fabric, then sucked. Her knees went weak and she held on to his shoulders so she wouldn't topple over. Parker wrapped his other arm around her waist, steadying her as he tugged the material aside and tasted her skin. He swirled his tongue around her painfully tight nipple.

"I've imagined this moment so many times," he muttered between licks and sucks that made her increasingly hot for him.

Just when she thought she'd combust, he pulled aside the fabric and released her other breast, lavishing it with the same attention.

Her legs shook and her breath came in quick, shallow pants that made her slightly light-headed. Suddenly he gazed up at her. There was something warm and liquid in his eyes. Like warm maple syrup.

God, the things I could do with a warm bottle of maple syrup right now.

Parker backed her up until her legs bumped the edge of one of the sturdy poolside lounge chairs. He lay her down and pressed his warm mouth to hers. One hand skimmed down her side, then slipped beneath her skirt.

He squeezed her bottom, most of which was exposed by panties that straddled the line between a thong and a brief. Kayleigh drew in a deep breath, breaking their kiss when he palmed the space between her thighs. Parker's gaze met hers, his nostrils flaring.

"Damn," he muttered, evidently pleased by the indisputable evidence of her desire for him.

Any lingering hesitancy between them dissipated.

Parker claimed her mouth in another bruising kiss. A steady pulse built in her core and her breath hitched as he teased the bundle of nerves and the sensitized flesh surrounding it.

"Parker, please. I need you," she whispered, hating the truth of those words as much as she anticipated the fulfillment of them.

He dragged the damp fabric down and off her legs with urgency.

Kayleigh released a soft cry when he plunged his fingers deep inside her and curled them, allowing him to reach the spot where she needed him so desperately.

Her breathy sighs came faster and her head lolled back as the overwhelming sensation built inside her like a storm growing in intensity. When he added the sensation of his thumb gliding across her sensitive nub and slick, swollen folds, her legs trembled from the intense pleasure.

Her stomach clenched and her core convulsed. Kayleigh squeezed her eyes shut as she rode the wave of pleasure that left her quivering and aching for more.

She heaved a sigh, her eyes drifting open.

Parker lay beside her. One edge of his sensuous mouth quirked in a half-smile that sent a prickle of heat to her already aching nipples.

"That was incredible." She sheepishly met his gaze. "But what would be even better is…" Kayleigh loosened his belt buckle. Her pulse pounded in her ears as she inched his zipper down.

Black boxer briefs.

She wouldn't have expected anything else from Parker Abbott. Kayleigh licked her lower lip as she studied the bulge in his shorts from its base to the damp circle over its tip.

Kayleigh swallowed hard, her heart beating wildly as she ran her fingertips along the fabric shielding him. She pressed soft kisses to his chest as she slipped her hand beneath his waistband and wrapped her fingers around his thick shaft.

Parker's eyes drifted shut. A shudder rolled up his spine as Kayleigh's hand glided up and down his length.

He took slow, measured breaths, each descending into a throaty exhalation. Though he realized it was impossible, it felt as if his heart would pound right out of his chest as she brought him closer to the edge.

It was a hand job, and he wasn't some hormone-filled teenage boy. But Kayleigh Jemison made him crazy with want. Everything about her stoked a fire deep inside him. In her absence, he felt a deep ache in his chest. In her presence, he was overcome by an overwhelming hunger for her. And what she was doing to him at the moment might drive him over the brink.

His urgent need for her was irrational and very much unlike him.

He prided himself on staying cool, being logical and maintaining self-control, even if he couldn't control the circumstances around him. But Kayleigh had a talent for shattering that.

He'd come to the cabin determined to be on his best behavior. To keep their relationship strictly business. His resolve had been hanging on by a worn thread all weekend. When she'd kissed him, every remaining ounce of it had disintegrated.

Parker met Kayleigh's gaze, hazy with lust. Needing another taste of her sweet, warm lips, he kissed her with a desperation that felt foreign, and yet deeply satisfying. He swept his tongue inside her mouth, savoring her kiss. Her hand continued to pump his shaft, the sensation building until he could barely hold on another moment.

Grasping her wrist, Parker stilled Kayleigh's hand. He dragged his mouth from hers, his breathing ragged. It required every ounce of determination he could muster to hold on. That hadn't happened since he'd been a bumbling teenage boy learning to navigate sex and the female body.

"You don't like it?" Kayleigh looked hurt and confused. An expression he knew well. It had been burned into his brain for the past two decades.

"No, that is definitely not the issue." His cheeks and forehead stung with heat.

"Oh." Her eyes widened with realization.

"I just thought you'd rather…" He indicated the chaise. "You know."

"Have sex?" Kayleigh seemed amused by his avoidance of the word. Her eyes twinkled as she stared at him intensely and smiled. "I would. I assume you have a condom in your wallet."

"Actually, a wallet isn't an ideal place to keep them. It's much safer to store them in—"

"Parker." Kayleigh's tone was sharp. "Do you have one?"

"I do."

"Could you get it? Like now?"

"Of course." He pressed an awkward kiss to her cheek and trotted upstairs to retrieve the strip of condoms from his shaving kit.

Parker caught a glimpse of himself in the mirror. He was shirtless, his cheeks were red and his pants were unfastened.

He enjoyed sex as much as the next guy, but what set him apart from his libido-driven counterparts had always been his ability to exercise logic and good sense.

At the moment, he was employing neither.

Sleeping with Kayleigh was a thrilling prospect. She was sexy and beautiful. Maddening, yet amusing. And he admired the hell out of her for her strength and tenacity. But the deal between Kayleigh and King's Finest was the most important thing in his world. And this could ruin everything.

He'd be taking one hell of a risk. A risk neither of them could afford.

This deal was too important to everyone involved.

Parker gripped the edge of the counter and cursed. *Kayleigh.*

She'd be madder than a wet hen. But it was the right

decision. He was sure of it. Hopefully when she calmed down, she'd come to the same conclusion. Maybe she'd even be glad he'd stopped them from taking this any further.

Parker's steps felt leaden as he returned to the spot where Kayleigh waited for him partially undressed. A sight he'd never forget.

Kayleigh studied him as he walked toward her. Her expression went from a soft, hazy lust to one he could read quite easily.

Animosity.

"You've changed your mind, haven't you?"

"Kayleigh, I'm sorry. I just think—"

"Save it, Parker. *Why* doesn't matter." Her cheeks flushed as she scrambled to her feet quickly. She tugged her skirt and bra back into place.

He stooped and retrieved both of their shirts from the stone floor and handed Kayleigh hers.

"God, I'm such an idiot." She swiped the garment from his hand and slipped it over her head. "I can't believe I did this, that I thought you…" She stopped short. Her gaze was filled with resentment.

Kayleigh searched the floor. Presumably in search of the black lace panties he'd stripped her of earlier.

Parker spotted them beneath the chaise. But before he could retrieve them, she'd stormed off toward her room, saying she'd be leaving in an hour, with or without him.

He was surprised she hadn't shoved him into the pool. After stooping to pick up her panties, he shoved them into his pocket and then dropped onto the chaise.

Kayleigh wasn't the idiot. He was.

He wanted to be with her. Desperately. But there was one thing he wanted more: to be named the next CEO of King's Finest.

Sleeping with Kayleigh Jemison could put his chances of that in serious jeopardy.

They were nearly back to his house and Kayleigh had barely uttered two words, other than "You drive," as she'd chucked the keys at him, narrowly missing his head.

Slumped against her seat, and wearing a faded T-shirt and tattered jeans, she'd spent the entire drive either staring out the window or scrolling through her phone.

"Kayleigh." Parker said her name softly as the car idled at a light. "I'm sorry, but it just wouldn't be prudent for either of us to jeopardize this deal. It has such large implications for both of us. The exposure was just too great."

She snapped her attention in his direction. "Seriously, Parker, are you trying really hard to be a dick, or does it just come naturally to you?"

"I don't under—"

"Of course you don't." She waved her hand dismissively. "Look, forget it. It was third base, not a marriage proposal. So let's pretend it never happened."

"Do people over twenty still say *third base*?" The light changed and he pulled off.

"God, you can be so…infuriating." She clenched her fists as she drew in a deep breath and released it, lowering her voice. "I asked you to drive because I was afraid that if I did, I'd be tempted to pull over and dump your body in a ditch. Now, please, just let it go. You learned how to dance and we're ready for the event next week. That's all that matters."

"So, the deal is still on?"

"It's like you said—it's too important to both of us." Kayleigh tossed her phone on the dashboard. "I didn't appreciate it at the time, but you're right. Sex would only complicate the deal. Neither of us needs that. So we each fulfill our end of the bargain and we walk away. No regrets."

Parker nodded as he turned onto the street that led to his neighborhood. He was glad Kayleigh recognized the logic of his decision. But she was wrong about one thing. Despite knowing all the reasons he shouldn't be with Kayleigh, he deeply regretted not making love to her.

It was a chance he'd never have again.

Thirteen

Kayleigh sifted through spools of jewelry wire stored in her studio supply room. She had another idea for the new line of jewelry she was designing, based on her weekend stay at the cabin with Parker.

The sun had gone down, but her mind still buzzed with ideas. She'd already made a few necklaces with matching bracelets and earrings, but another design was knocking around in her head, if only she could find that damn sheet of pink lace variegated brass leaf. It would create beautiful contrasts on another design that would be ideal for fall.

"Kayleigh."

She dropped the spools of copper and silver wire and nearly toppled the cabinet. Parker was standing in the doorway between the shop and the back room.

"Parker? What the—"

"I didn't mean to scare you." He held his hands up in surrender. "I worked late tonight and decided to grab a bite to eat before the pizza shop closed. I noticed your light was still on in the studio."

Kayleigh retrieved the spool of copper wire from the floor and Parker held out the roll of silver wire, which had rolled to his feet.

"Thanks." She accepted the spool, then quickly turned and shoved it back into the bin. "Is there something you need?"

"No, I just…well, they were offering a deal on the extra-large pizzas that didn't seem prudent to pass up, but it's more than I can eat alone. I thought maybe…" He shifted his weight from one foot to the other, looking as uncomfortable as she'd felt the night he'd left her half naked on that chaise and suddenly decided he didn't want to sleep with her.

Good.

It didn't begin to make up for the humiliation she'd felt in that moment. She considered herself confident, but a rejection like that could take a hammer to even the most self-assured woman's ego.

"You thought maybe…*what*?" Kayleigh folded her arms, eyeing him impatiently. She was eager to get back to searching for materials for her project.

"I thought maybe you'd like to split it with me." Parker unbuttoned the top button of his crisp white shirt and loosened his navy printed tie before shoving a hand into the pocket of slim, gray pants that seemed tailored to his lean, muscular frame. "Have you eaten dinner yet?"

"No." She'd nibbled on a granola bar she discovered in a drawer five hours earlier. "Pizza would be great. I can grab a plate from upstairs if you want to leave me a couple of slices."

She searched through the cabinet for the metal leaf again.

"I guess I didn't explain myself very well. I thought maybe we could eat *together*." Parker squatted beside Cricket, who'd walked over to greet him. He rubbed her ears and ruffled the fur on either side of her head. Cricket looked uncommonly content.

Traitor.

"I'm working still." Kayleigh gave Cricket a side-eye before rummaging in the cabinet again.

"Then we could have a working dinner. Right here." He gestured toward her work space.

"Look, Parker, if this is a pity thing, it's completely unnecessary." She turned to him, her arms folded. "That thing that didn't happen between us? I've put it out of my mind."

"This isn't a pity thing." Parker's cheeks flushed. "It just didn't make sense to waste half of a perfectly good Hawaiian pizza—"

"You ordered Hawaiian pizza?" She raised a brow. "I thought you said ham and pineapple on a pizza was disgusting."

Parker shrugged. "I tried a slice. Just to prove to myself that it was as awful as I thought."

"And?"

"It was one of the best damn pizzas I've ever eaten," he conceded with a half smile.

"Fine." Kayleigh huffed, sure she'd soon regret her decision. "If you don't mind me working while we eat."

"Of course not. I'll grab the pizza from the car." He opened the door and turned back toward her. "When you're working late like this, you really should lock your door."

"We live in Mayberry," she scoffed. "Nothing remotely interesting ever happens here."

"Even in Mayberry there was crime," he countered.

She folded her arms again, her jaw tight. "If I'd locked the door tonight, I wouldn't be having this conversation about locking the door with you now. So there is that to consider."

He pressed his lips together and his mouth curved in a partial smile. "Don't lock me out, in case you were considering it."

"Of course not." She *totally* was. "How else would I get my Hawaiian pizza?"

"Maybe I was just incredibly hungry, but Margot's pizza was exceptional tonight," Kayleigh declared after unapologetically polishing off her third slice.

"It's her new chef," he confirmed. "I've noticed subtle improvements in their menu since she hired him."

Awkward silence stretched between them for a few moments. Kayleigh couldn't take it anymore. She stood suddenly and wiped her hands on a napkin.

"Thank you for the pizza, Parker. But I need to get back to work, and I still haven't found that metal leaf.

Besides, I'm sure there's something else you'd rather be doing tonight."

Parker didn't acknowledge her polite and apparently too subtle attempt at saying *you don't have to go home, but you've gotta get the hell out of here*. He walked over to the storage cabinet she'd been searching. "How do you ever find anything in here?"

"I generally know where everything is." Maybe she wasn't as organized as him, but she had a system. Sort of.

"What were you looking for?"

Kayleigh described the thin metal sheets she was searching for and Parker helped her go through the shelves, which were overflowing with jewelry-making components.

"Is this it?" Parker held up a shipping envelope from the company that supplied her metal leaf.

"Yes! Thanks. I could kiss you right now." She took the envelope from him excitedly. Then, realizing what she'd said, she added, "Don't flip out—it's just an expression. You're in no danger of me kissing you again. *Believe me*." She muttered the last part under her breath.

"I understand." Parker frowned and shoved his hands back in his pockets.

"Well, thank you for dinner and for helping me find this." Kayleigh held up the envelope after an uncomfortable lull between them. "I'd better get back to work."

Parker nodded, but didn't move toward the door. "I'd love to see what you're working on."

She furrowed her brow, her head cocked as she studied him for a moment. "Why?"

"I thought I'd get an early start on shopping for my mother's birthday this year. I'd love to get a first look at your newest designs."

Kayleigh seemed to find his response reasonable. She directed him to an arrangement of three necklaces with matching bracelets and earrings.

"These are incredible, Kayleigh." He studied the pieces, one by one. Using gold-and-silver wire, she'd recreated some of the flowers and leaves they'd seen during their hike. Each piece was more stunning than the last. The third set was embellished with precious stones.

"This one is particularly beautiful." He admired the wire-wrapped stones and her intricate work. "I'd never really noticed what exceptional work you do. I'd like to buy this set."

"I'm not quite finished with it, and I'm not sure how much I'll charge for it when I'm done."

"Well, when you decide, I'd like it." He shoved his hands in his pockets.

Kayleigh narrowed her gaze at him and then waved her hand. "Consider it a gift."

She was wearing tattered jeans and an old T-shirt. Her hair was pulled high in a lopsided bun that a light breeze could've blown apart. Yet he could barely take his eyes off her. And he couldn't stop thinking of the taste of her mouth or how it had felt to hold her in his arms.

"No, I couldn't."

"You paid for the upgrade to the cabin and King's Finest is covering my travel expenses this weekend." She swept aside a few stray curls that had tumbled free of her loose bun. "It's the least I can do."

"You let me know when you decide on a price for that set." He didn't acknowledge her offer again as he turned to leave. "Be sure to lock the door this time." He gave her a faint smile. "Good night, Kayleigh."

She followed him to the door, wished him a good night and locked it behind him.

Parker squeezed his eyes shut against the vision of Kayleigh at the cabin that day, wishing he'd made a different choice.

Fourteen

Kayleigh studied herself in the full-length mirror. Her hotel room was gorgeous, as was the hotel where Parker's national distillery trade organization was holding their conference and gala. He'd arrived earlier in the week, while she'd arrived the previous day.

Parker had planned a day of sightseeing for them, and as much as she hated to admit it, it had been fun. She'd been to New York before, with Aidan, but she hadn't visited any of the touristy sites like the Empire State Building or the Statue of Liberty. Which was something she'd mentioned to Parker when he'd proposed this trip.

He'd arranged for her to visit both, and earlier that day they'd gone on one of those cheesy television-show tours. She'd loved every minute of it. And despite himself, Parker seemed to enjoy it, too. He'd been genuinely disappointed when she had other plans for lunch.

She raked her manicured fingernails through her shiny, silken coppery curls and tugged her hair over one shoulder, hoping he'd be pleased when he discovered how she'd spent the afternoon.

Kayleigh removed her dress from its silk hanger and stepped into the soft, buttery gold satin, sliding it up her body. The floor-length dress had a deep V-neck, a low-cut back, spaghetti straps and a thigh-high slit.

It wasn't something she'd typically wear, but Savannah had gotten teary-eyed when she'd tried the dress on and insisted that this was the one. So Kayleigh had trusted her hormonal friend and ventured outside of her comfort zone.

There was a knock at the door that separated her hotel room from Parker's.

"Perfect timing." She opened the door and turned her back toward him. "Can you get this zipper for me?"

Parker set something down, then zipped up her dress. "Kayleigh, you look…absolutely stunning."

"Thank you." She surveyed his charcoal gray Michael Kors tuxedo and pristine white tuxedo shirt. "You look quite handsome, too. Except…"

She adjusted his black bow tie a smidge. It was the kind of thing that she normally didn't notice, but would drive Parker insane. "Perfect."

"Ready?" He checked his watch. A Bvlgari with a black alligator strap, an eighteen-karat rose-gold bezel and a transparent dial that revealed its black gears. The watch had to be worth more than her truck. Maybe even when it was new.

"Yes." Kayleigh stepped into the gold, peep toe Betsey Johnson stilettos she'd picked out to go with the dress. The four-inch heels were studded with crystals and had an ankle strap. She picked up her cell phone. It was all she planned to carry.

"Before we go…" Parker retrieved the box he'd set down when he'd zipped her dress. It was wrapped in shiny gold paper and had an organza bow. He handed it to her. "This is for you."

"What is it?" Kayleigh studied the beautiful box. It was almost too pretty to open.

He shrugged. "Only one way to find out."

Kayleigh carefully loosened the bow, set the box on the bed and opened it. She gasped. "This is the Alexander McQueen clutch I admired in the shop window yesterday. You went back for it?"

He shrugged, as if buying her a bag that cost more than her mortgage payment was no big deal. "You liked it, and you said you didn't have a handbag for a formal event."

Kayleigh glided her fingers over the crystal-studded black calf leather and the hinged clasp with its signature skull and embellished four-ring knuckle-duster. "Parker, this was incredibly sweet of you, but it's much too expensive a gift. Besides, I thought you didn't like it."

"I didn't at first. But the more I thought about it, the more I understood why you love it. It's edgy, yet beautiful. Classic, yet modern. It suits you, Kayleigh." He lifted the black leather clutch from the box and extended it to her. "So I want you to have it. It's that simple."

Parker Abbott was an enigma she might never understand. He could be infuriating, but he could also be sweet and insightful. "I don't know what to say other than…thank you."

She pressed a quick kiss to his cheek, then wiped off the smudge of lipstick left in its wake.

They made their way down to the beautifully appointed ballroom. Kayleigh tensed the moment they stepped inside. Most of the women were dripping with diamonds and wearing expensive, high-end designer ball gowns. Many were wearing red-bottomed heels.

She'd felt confident and beautiful when she'd stepped on that elevator, but now she felt like she was on the JV team when everyone else here was clearly varsity.

Parker slipped an arm around her waist. "You'll do fine, and you look amazing." He guided her to their table and pulled out her chair. "Can I get you a drink?"

"A dirty martini, please."

"Coming right up."

Kayleigh watched Parker walk across the room. He looked incredibly handsome in his tuxedo and there was something about the swagger of his walk that…

No. Nope. Stop it.

Kayleigh reminded herself of all the reasons she shouldn't be thinking of Parker Abbott that way.

Parker surveyed the crowded room as he moved toward the bar. He reached inside his tuxedo jacket for his wallet when the bartender requested his order. "A manhattan and a dirty martini, please."

"I hope that dirty martini is for me," a sultry voice whispered in his ear.

"Elena." His spine stiffened as he turned to face her. "How are you?"

"Better now that you're here." Her brown eyes twinkled.

Elena Mixon was the kind of woman who commanded attention anywhere she went. The kind of woman that just about any man would want on his arm. But Elena was no man's arm candy. Nor would she ever consent to being a trophy wife. Much to the chagrin of her parents.

She was as dedicated and driven as any man he'd ever met, and like him, she was determined to prove that she was the one who should be running her family's distillery. An opinion her old-school father, traditional mother and six siblings—five of whom were male— heartily disagreed with.

"And I was afraid it was going to be boring this year." She trailed a finger down his arm, her brown eyes gleaming.

They'd last seen each other at an event two years ago. And they'd seen every inch of each other.

"Actually, I brought a date this year."

She smacked her lips as if it were the most preposterous thing she'd ever heard. "I thought you didn't believe in dating."

"Generally speaking." He shoved one hand in his pocket and leaned against the bar.

"What makes this girl so special?"

"She just…is." Parker glanced in Kayleigh's direction. Their eyes met and she smiled. It warmed something in his chest.

He checked his watch. *What the hell is taking the bartender so long with those drinks?*

"How long have you two been dating?" Elena parked herself on the stool beside him.

Parker groaned quietly. Elena was worse than he was at taking hints. "Not long, but we have history. We were best friends in grade school."

"And what prompted the change in your relationship?"

"Is there a reason you're so interested in my love life?"

"The thing is, I didn't think you had a love life. That's why I didn't press for anything more than industry-event hookups. But when you change the rules of the game, darling, it isn't fair to not inform the other players." Elena crossed her legs and one long, shapely leg peeked through the high slit of her dress.

"We haven't seen each other in two years. You're upset because I'm here with someone else?" He was honestly baffled by Elena's reaction. "Why? Neither of us expressed an interest in a relationship."

Elena sighed. "I understand, but if I'd known there was another option—"

"Another option for what?"

"Don't play coy with me. You know good and well that—"

"Hi, babe. I thought I'd check on our drinks." Kayleigh suddenly appeared beside him, her clutch in hand.

He blinked. Had she just called him *babe*?

"Parker can be so…well, you know…Parker." Kayleigh smiled at Elena. "Hi, I'm Kayleigh Jemison. I'm Parker's—"

"Fiancée." The word escaped his mouth abruptly, taking all three of them by surprise.

"Fiancée?" Elena echoed.

"Yes." Kayleigh stared up at him lovingly, after quickly recovering from her initial shock at his sudden declaration. "I'm his fiancée."

"But no engagement ring?" Elena tapped her long fingernails against the oak bar.

Parker and Kayleigh exchanged glances. It was something they hadn't considered.

"I'm a jewelry designer, so I'm hard to shop for." Kayleigh smiled at Elena sweetly. "But I'm confident we'll find the right ring."

"Yes." Parker wrapped his arm around Kayleigh's waist and pulled her closer. "I know we will, sweetheart."

She wasn't the only one who could throw around terms of endearment.

After an awkward silence between them, Parker spoke. "My apologies, ladies. I should've introduced you from the outset. Kayleigh, this is Elena Mixon. Her family owns Mixon Whiskey. And Elena, you already know that Kayleigh Jemison is—"

"Your fiancée." Elena sounded completely unconvinced.

"It's a pleasure to meet you, Elena." Kayleigh nodded, then turned toward the bartender, who'd finally brought their drinks and apologized for the delay.

"What was that about?" Kayleigh asked once they'd taken their leave and returned to their table. "The look you gave me… I could tell you needed an escape from your friend over there, but I didn't expect you to pull the whole fiancée thing out of the hat."

"Neither did I." Parker gulped his drink. He still wasn't sure why he'd said it. But if the encounter with Elena was any indication, their fake-fiancée experiment was going to go up in flames before they unmoored the boat from the dock.

"I guess it's only fair." Kayleigh sipped her martini. "You're playing my fake fiancé for a week—the least I can do is play yours for one night." She set her martini down. "It's good this happened. Elena brought up a very good point."

"The ring. I know. I hadn't thought of that either."

"I cannot go there with a fake ring. Aidan's mother and sister would spot it from a mile away. Maybe I can find a really nice ring at a pawn shop here."

"Don't worry about the ring." Parker swigged his manhattan, then set the glass on the table. "I've got that covered. A friend owes me a favor."

"Thank you, Parker."

The relief and gratitude in Kayleigh's eyes made him sit a bit taller. He liked being someone she could count on.

"Parker, it's so good to see you."

He stood as Malcolm and Sarah Mays, the owners of

a gin distillery in Washington State, joined them at the table. He accepted a hug from the kindly older woman and then shook her husband's hand.

"And you must be Parker's fiancée." The woman grinned.

Kayleigh nearly choked on her martini. She set her glass down and gave him a panicked look before her smile fell back into place. "Yes, ma'am. It's a pleasure to meet you."

Parker searched the room for Elena. She was talking with a group of industry execs and pointing in their direction.

By the time the night was over, the entire room would know.

Fifteen

"You've been practicing." Kayleigh looked up at Parker as they swayed together on the dance floor. She was surprised at how light and confident his steps were.

"I'll neither confirm nor deny." He chuckled. "Maybe I just had a really good teacher."

"Well, that's for sure." She grinned. There was a beat of silence between them before she blurted out, "I'm sorry this whole fiancé thing got out of control. I should've stayed at our table and let you handle your friend over there."

"It isn't your fault. I'm the one who told her. I just didn't think she'd make it her mission to tell everyone here."

Kayleigh's cheeks heated. They'd been congratulated by countless distillery owners and execs, as well as several of the vendors. And more than once the photographer had asked to take a picture of the award winner and his fiancée. Photos that would hopefully go into a single email or, better yet, be buried on someone's hard drive.

"Congrats again on the award." Kayleigh was anxious to change the subject. "Your acceptance speech was heartfelt and witty. You even made us laugh. I was impressed." She grinned. "I know your family is enjoying themselves in the Caribbean, but it's too bad they couldn't be here to see you tonight."

"Thankfully I wasn't alone."

There was something so warm and open about his expression. It caught her off guard and made her belly do a little flip. Suddenly she was keenly aware of the placement of his large hand low on her back and how their bodies moved together. It stirred up all of the feelings that had led her to kiss him that day at the cabin. Something she couldn't stop thinking about, no matter how hard she tried.

This is a business arrangement. Real feelings have no place in a fake relationship. Because the only person who would get hurt was her. Again. Parker would go on with his life as if nothing had happened. Experience had taught her that.

"Everything okay?" Parker frowned.

"Yes." She stopped swaying and took a step away from him. "It's been a long day."

"And it's been a long week for me." Parker looked disappointed, though he managed a cursory smile.

"We stayed a socially acceptable amount of time, and I danced. Seems like a good time to call it a night."

Kayleigh forced a smile and slipped her arm through his, disappointed that their weekend together was coming to an end.

Kayleigh said good-night to Parker and closed the door behind her. She pressed her back against the cool door and sighed. Just a few more weeks and then they could go back to the way things were. Hopefully she and Parker wouldn't be enemies. But they wouldn't need to spend time together, either.

She tossed her clutch on the bed and kicked off her heels. Her feet ached, and she remembered exactly why she preferred a broken-in pair of cowboy boots.

A knock at the door between their rooms startled her. She swung the door open.

"Yes?"

Parker didn't speak right away. He just stared at her for a moment. "Need help with that zipper again?"

"Oh, yes. Thanks." Kayleigh tried to tamp down the disappointment in her voice. She turned her back to him and swept her hair over one shoulder.

He stepped forward and slowly unzipped the back of her dress. When he was done, he didn't move and neither did she. Kayleigh stood there, heart racing, the sound of her heartbeat filling her ears.

Parker slipped his arms around her waist and pulled her against him as he leaned down and kissed her neck.

Kayleigh's eyes drifted closed at the delicious sensation of his lips grazing her heated skin. She relaxed against Parker's hard chest and felt his heart thudding against her back.

She allowed her head to fall back, granting him complete access to her neck and bare shoulder. Her entire body shivered as he planted soft kisses along her skin.

A soft murmur escaped her mouth when Parker's hand glided up the front of her body and cupped her breast. She leaned into his touch, wanting more.

He turned her around and captured her mouth in an intense kiss. One hand was pressed to the heated skin of her bare back; the other was wrapped around her waist, pulling their lower bodies closer.

Kayleigh slid her hands beneath his jacket and wrapped her arms around his back, desperate for more contact between them. Parker obliged. His strong hands eased down her body, gripped her bottom and hauled her against him. His growing length was pinned between them.

Kayleigh's eyes opened abruptly at the memory of the humiliation she'd felt when Parker had suddenly changed his mind. She couldn't do that again. And there was no way their business relationship could recover from it a second time.

She did have a modicum of pride.

Kayleigh pulled away and shook her head. "No, Parker. You don't get to do this to me again. You made it clear that it's a bad idea for us to sleep together. Have you changed your mind?"

Parker frowned. "Assessing the situation objectively, I know it's risky."

Kayleigh's cheeks burned. Her fingers drifted to her lips. "Then why'd you—"

"Because I want you, Kayleigh." He planted his hands loosely on her hips, his intense gaze pinning her in place. "I can't stop thinking about you or that night. I can't stop wishing I'd made a different choice. For once in my life, I don't give a damn about doing what's logical. I just know I want this…that I want you."

Kayleigh's hands trembled slightly. She sucked in a deep breath and slipped one strap then the other from her shoulder. The silky material glided onto the floor.

Parker's mouth twisted in a sexy grin when she gripped the lapels of his jacket and pulled him down for another kiss.

The fire grew in his belly and spread through his limbs as Parker kissed Kayleigh, palming her round bottom and hauling her against him. His body was strung tightly with a desperate need for this woman. Thoughts of Kayleigh filled his head constantly now, distracting him from his work during the day and keeping him awake at night.

He kissed her with a hunger that she seemed to feel, too. Until they were both gasping for breath.

Kayleigh pulled away, her chest heaving and her warm brown eyes studying his.

Parker hoped to God that Kayleigh wasn't having a moment of clarity. Because for the first time in a very long time, he didn't care about logic and reason. He simply wanted to give into the sensations that overwhelmed him whenever he was with this woman.

He wanted to feel the heat raging between her luscious thighs as her molten center pressed against him. Her soft breasts, with their pointed peaks, mashing against his hard chest. Her warm hands on his hot skin. Her lips crushed against his. The sense of urgency and the enthralling feeling of spinning out of control.

He was addicted to that feeling and to her. And he didn't want it to stop.

Kayleigh slipped her hand in his and led him to the bed. She helped him out of his tuxedo jacket and dropped it onto the chair before slowly unbuttoning his shirt.

He couldn't take his eyes off her gorgeous face and the deep flush of her cheeks as her fingers nimbly pushed each button through its hole.

As sexy as she was, slowly undressing him, he desperately wanted to kiss her again and glide his hands over her bare skin. And he ached to be buried deep inside her.

Parker stripped off his shirt and pants, hastily retrieving the strip of foil packets he'd shoved into his pocket before he'd knocked on Kayleigh's door. He dropped them onto the bedside table.

"Ambitious." Kayleigh's mouth pulled into a playful grin as she regarded the strip of six condoms.

Parker was neither bashful nor prudish. Yet, somehow, Kayleigh had a gift for making him blush, and she seemed to take great delight in it.

"I wasn't sure that would be enough."

Kayleigh grinned, her eyes twinkling. She sank her

teeth into her luscious lower lip, then lifted onto her toes and pressed a kiss to his eager mouth.

Parker cradled her face as he savored the taste of her sweet lips and the sensation of her tongue gliding against his. He could hold this woman in his arms and kiss her until the sky turned green and the grass turned blue. And still it would never be enough.

He lay her on the bed and hovered over her, his gaze meeting hers. His heart pounded so loudly that the sound seemed to fill the space around him.

Parker wanted to tell Kayleigh everything he'd been thinking these past few weeks. That he cared for her deeply. That he often wished he could go back to that day when they were kids and make a different choice. That he'd do anything to take away the pain she'd suffered during their years apart. But the words lodged in his throat. He stared at her without a word.

Kayleigh traced his cheekbone with her thumb, her eyes drifting closed as she pressed her mouth to his again. He kissed her; this time the kiss was slow and sweet even as heat built between them.

Parker stripped Kayleigh of her pretty black lace strapless bra and matching panties before chucking his boxers, ripping open one of the little foil squares and sheathing himself.

He kissed his way down her chest, flicking her hardened nipple with his tongue. His body tensed in response to her sensual murmur.

There was something so incredibly provocative about Kayleigh. She was sexy, regardless of whether she was wearing a satin gown or tattered jeans and a tee. And she could get a rise out of him like no one else. She'd been the source of joy, anger, frustration and amusement. But lately the feelings Kayleigh engendered in him most were a consuming lust and an affection that grew deeper with every passing day.

This moment was everything he'd dreamed of, and he couldn't wait another minute to be inside her.

Parker guided himself to her entrance, his hips inching forward. Everything about this woman made him feel incredible in a way he hadn't experienced before. His senses were overwhelmed with pleasure intensified by her soft whimpers.

A delicious sensation rolled up his spine as he glided inside her, slowly and deliberately. He was intent on savoring every moment of their connection.

Kayleigh wrapped her arms around him, her freshly manicured nails digging into his back as he circled his hips with focused determination.

He alternated deep and shallow thrusts, allowing her responses to guide him until she tensed, her body trembling as she called his name.

His pulse raced and beads of perspiration trickled down his back as her inner walls contracted around his heated flesh. Parker cursed beneath his breath, his back tensing as he found his release with a few more thrusts.

Parker collapsed on the bed beside her, both of them still breathing heavily. There were so many things he wanted to say to Kayleigh. But instead, he gave her a quick kiss and made his way to the bathroom.

It'd been a long time since he'd been in a relationship. Sex had simply been a biological need. A necessary mutual release. But with Kayleigh, everything felt…different.

He wasn't sure exactly what their sleeping together meant for their relationship. Or what her expectations were. It was something they should have addressed prior to having sex. He'd known that, but it wasn't the head above his shoulders that had won the argument. Which meant they needed to talk about it now.

But when he returned from the bathroom, Kayleigh lay on her side with her back to him. Her rhythmic breathing indicated that she'd fallen asleep.

Parker sighed, relieved they could delay the awkward *what-does-this-mean-for-us* conversation for another day. But it presented another problem. Did he go back to his own room, as he typically would? Or should he crawl into bed beside her?

Neither option seemed quite right.

Parker sat in the chair beside Kayleigh's bed as she slept. He'd checked his email, worked on some spreadsheets and watched a couple of financial news shows. He'd even managed to doze off to sleep.

"Parker?" Kayleigh rolled over, her hand searching the empty spot he'd vacated hours earlier.

"I'm here."

She turned toward him and then sat up in bed. "Did you sleep in that chair all night?"

"I needed to catch up on some work, and I didn't want to wake you."

"Then why didn't you return to your room?" She eyed him suspiciously.

"I thought you'd find it rude if I just left," he admitted. "The chair was a compromise."

A slow smile curled one edge of her mouth, and her eyes twinkled as if she was pleased with his answer. She yawned and ran her hands through her wild red curls. When she spotted the time—barely five o'clock in the morning—she extended a hand to him.

"It's too early to do anything. You're on vacation."

"Actually, it's a business trip."

"Parker." She wiggled her fingers. "Come to bed."

He set his phone on the table and stood, taking a deep breath before he slid beneath the covers and wrapped an arm around her.

They were both quiet for a moment. Kayleigh raised her head and met his gaze. "Look, I know you're probably freaking out because you think this means we're suddenly...I don't know...a couple or something. It doesn't. We're two sensible adults and this is just... sex. I'm not looking for anything more than this."

"Oh, okay." He wasn't sure whether he should feel relieved or slighted by her declaration.

"But since we've broken that barrier... I'd certainly be open to doing this again. Since you've still got a few left and all." Kayleigh glanced at the foil packets on the nightstand and then grinned. She pressed her open palm to his chest, halting his movement when he reached for them. "After I get a few more hours of sleep and a shower."

"Deal." Parker grinned, lying back down and propping one arm behind his head.

"Parker, can I ask you something?" Kayleigh folded her arms over his chest and propped her chin on her hands. "Are you planning a hostile takeover of King's Finest?"

"What would make you think that?" He frowned.

"I noticed the research you were reviewing when I joined you for breakfast this morning. It was about merit-based family-owned business succession as opposed to succession based on birth order." She tilted her head as she regarded him. "You're trying to leapfrog Blake as the next CEO, aren't you?"

"Yes. Because I think it's in our company's best interest." He stared at the ceiling. "And it wouldn't be a hostile takeover. It would be by consensus. I plan to prove that I'm the best candidate for the position."

"And that's why you were willing to do this. Playing my fake fiancé for the sake of your family's deal...it's a perfect opportunity to prove to your father that you should be the heir apparent." She lay on her back in the crook of his arm.

There was silence between them for a few moments. "You think I'm being unfair to Blake?"

"I think he deserves to know how you feel and so do Max and Zora."

"I plan to tell them, but I wanted to wait until after my parents' big anniversary party."

"In case your brothers and sister don't take the news too well?" Kayleigh laughed. "Because boy would that make the party *awkward*."

"Exactly." He couldn't help chuckling, too.

"Who have you told about this?"

"Just you." There was something oddly comforting about there being a secret that only the two of them shared. "Hey, what do you think about switching to a later flight, if one is available? There's a little gallery in West Chelsea that I'd love to take you to, if we have time."

"I'd like that." Kayleigh pressed her cheek to his chest and settled against him.

Parker pulled up the airline app and switched their tickets. Before he was done, Kayleigh had already fallen back to sleep. Her soft breath skittered across his chest as her limbs tangled with his.

Parker kissed the top of her head and readjusted his pillow as he stared at the ceiling of the hotel room. He wouldn't be leaving anytime soon, so he might as well settle in and enjoy having Kayleigh's warm, lush, naked body pressed to his.

Sixteen

Parker Abbott did something he never, ever did. He called the office, took the day off and slept in.

He and Kayleigh had returned to Magnolia Lake in the wee hours of the morning after taking a later flight back. Besides, between making love to Kayleigh and his insistence on sleeping in that damned chair, he'd gotten very little sleep. He usually subsisted on a few hours. But it needed to be three or four solid hours in a comfortable bed.

He awoke, showered and fixed himself breakfast, with thoughts of his night with Kayleigh still running through his head. Maybe sleeping with her was an ill-advised move, but it was one he couldn't bring himself to regret. In fact his only regret was not taking her to bed that night at the cabin.

Parker had made himself a late breakfast and was loading the dishwasher when his doorbell rang. He peeked through the small windows at the top of the ornate wood door.

"Mom?" Parker swung the door open and she rushed past him, not bothering to give him her traditional hug and kiss. He furrowed his brows and closed the door. "What's wrong? Did something happen at the office?"

"Yes." She looked both angry and teary. "How could you get engaged and announce it to the entire world without telling your own family?"

Shit.

He zeroed in on the sheet of paper she was waving, taking it from her hand. It was the e-newsletter from the trade organization that had put on the event they'd attended over the weekend. The caption under the lead photo proclaimed that the executive of the year was in attendance with his fiancée.

"Mom, I can explain."

Or could he? He couldn't tell his mother about the deal with Kayleigh. It would ruin the surprise his family had worked so hard on.

"I'm listening." Iris Abbott folded her arms and plopped down on the sofa in his great room. "I'd love to hear you explain why you'd tell the entire free world but couldn't be bothered to pick up the phone and share your happy news with your mother."

Parker sank onto the sofa and wrapped an arm around her.

"I told Elena Mixon that Kayleigh was my fiancée to make it clear that there was nothing between us. She made it her business to tell the entire association. Once it spread like wildfire…well… I couldn't very well change my story."

"So you and Kayleigh *aren't* engaged?" His mother seemed disappointed when he confirmed that they weren't. "That's a shame. She's good for you, Parker."

"What makes you say that?" Parker sank against the back of the cushion. "We're like fire and ice. Polar opposites."

He actually wanted to believe that there could be something more to him and Kayleigh. That what they'd shared last night could be the beginning of something bigger instead of the end of their fake-fiancé experiment. But there was too much baggage between them, and they were too different in nature.

Wasn't that a recipe for disaster?

He cared too much for Kayleigh to hurt her any more than he already had.

"I guess you've never heard the old saying that opposites attract." His mother patted his knee.

"I have. It's filed in here—" he tapped his temple "—alongside stories of Sasquatch and alien abductions."

They both laughed when she elbowed him.

"Seriously, Mom, if there's one thing I've learned about relationships from watching you and Dad, it's the importance of a unified purpose. You two have a lot in common. So do Blake and Savannah."

"But we have a lot of differences, too. That's what brings variety and interest to a relationship, sweetheart." Her eyes twinkled. "There's something special between you and Kayleigh. There always has been. It broke my heart when you two parted ways as kids. I've always hoped that one day you two would figure things out and fix your relationship. Good friendships are hard to come by."

Parker nodded. "I know, Mom. These past few weeks with her have been great. In some ways she's still the girl I've always known. In other ways I wonder if I ever really knew her or understood her situation at all."

"Well, whatever it is that you two have… I still see it in her eyes. You care deeply for her, Parker. And despite how hurt and angry she might be over what happened between you two, it appears that she has deep feelings for you, too."

"I don't know. Sometimes I look at her and I think… maybe we could be…something. But other times…" He sighed and ran a hand over his head.

"Life isn't like the data you love so much, honey." His mother's tone was soothing. "There's no guarantee that two plus two will equal four."

"Precisely. Data is reliable. Two plus two *always* equals four. And if you perform the steps correctly, the data can fairly accurately predict what you should expect. There are variables, but—"

"That's what makes life and love so exciting." She cut off his ramblings, a wide smile spread across her still-beautiful face. "Love is unpredictable. You never know exactly how things will turn out. You have to use your mind, your heart and your instincts to make the right decision when it comes to love."

"Who said anything about love?"

"Romance, relationships, affection. Whatever you want to call it." She waved a hand dismissively.

"The point is that numbers are straightforward. They don't confuse the hell out of you and make you doubt yourself."

His mother placed a gentle hand on his arm. "Maybe she's struggling with her feelings, too."

He hadn't considered that.

Maybe she was grappling with her feelings. Or maybe she'd meant exactly what she'd said. That he shouldn't read anything deeper into their sleeping together, because it was only temporary. Once he'd fulfilled the terms of their contract, they would go their separate ways.

Parker turned to face his mother. "If we were truly compatible, it wouldn't be such a struggle, would it?"

His mother frowned. "Things in life aren't always so straightforward, son. But the effort makes the reward sweeter. So if you truly care for Kayleigh and want a relationship with her—romantic or otherwise—be prepared to roll up your sleeves and work for it."

She didn't wait for his response. His mother kissed his cheek and walked to the door. "And don't be afraid to tell her how you feel. You might never get the chance to again."

Parker locked the door behind his mother and groaned. He was a man who valued order and control. He liked knowing what came next. More important, he liked being in control of what came next. And of his feelings. But with Kayleigh Jemison, he was never sure what came next or of how she'd make him feel.

A little part of Kayleigh seemed to relish slowly driving him insane and making him want things he shouldn't.

Yet all he could think about was cradling her in his arms and making her his again and again. Shattering her control and allowing her to decimate his.

Parker had monitored his voice mail, email and text messages all week.

No messages from Kayleigh.

It was week ten, their last date before they went away to her friend's destination wedding. It was Kayleigh's turn to choose the place, but she hadn't responded to his text asking where they were going.

Perhaps she'd chosen to skip it.

Regardless of where it began, every date they'd had since New York had ended with the two of them in bed. They'd made love in her hotel room in New York, in her storage room the night he helped her do inventory at her shop, and in his shower and bed after a movie and late-night swim at his place.

Well before that night in New York, he'd begun to anticipate their weekly dates. No matter how hard he tried to focus on work, he couldn't stop thinking of her smile, the sweet sound of her laugh or the way her creamy skin glided against his.

He wanted Kayleigh. Thought of her constantly. Was driven to distraction by her. But she didn't seem to be as affected by him.

He needed to renew his focus on the priority at hand. Proving to his father, and to his siblings, that he should be the next CEO of King's Finest Distillery. Getting sidetracked by the feelings he'd developed for Kayleigh Jemison was a mistake.

Still, it was Friday evening, and he couldn't help being disappointed that she'd chosen to blow off their final date.

Parker went to the bar overlooking the patio. He'd never be able to look at his pool again without remembering Kayleigh stripping naked, diving into the water and then inviting him to join her.

He dropped brown and white sugar cubes into a rock glass, added both orange and Angostura bitters and a splash of water, and then muddled it. Parker stirred in two ounces of King's Finest bourbon, then two large ice cubes. He finished it off with lemon and orange peel.

The perfect old-fashioned cocktail.

As Parker raised the glass to his mouth, he heard a car door slam. The doorbell rang and he answered it.

"Kayleigh, did I miss your message?"

"May I?" She indicated his glass and he handed the drink to her. Kayleigh took a gulp, her eyes fluttering closed for a moment. She sighed, handing the glass back to him. "I didn't send a text message or an email. I didn't know if I should say what I want to say."

"Come in." He stepped aside and invited her to have a seat on the sofa. Parker handed the glass back to her. "You look like you could use this more than me."

She nodded and took another sip before finally raising her eyes to meet his as he sat on the opposite sofa.

"This is our last date and all week I've tried to think of how I wanted to spend it." She walked over to stand in front of him, setting the glass down on a nearby coaster. "But I only want one thing." She straddled his lap and pressed a palm to his cheek. "I want to spend it making love to you."

Something in his chest fluttered and he felt an overwhelming sense of joy.

"I can't think of a better way to spend it." He cradled her cheek and pressed his lips to hers.

His tongue swept inside the warm cavern of her mouth; she tasted of sugar, citrus and the unique bourbon recipe that had built his family's fortune. He slid his hands up her back to remove her bra, but she wasn't wearing one.

Kayleigh lifted her arms, allowing him to pull the fabric over her head, revealing her firm breasts and hardened brown peaks.

He showered kisses down her neck and shoulder, palming one heavy globe before laving its pebbled tip with his tongue.

Kayleigh pressed her palm to the back of his head and ground her hips against him, causing him to harden painfully.

"You taste even better than I remembered," he whispered against her soft skin between gentle bites and leisurely licks.

"That's just the appetizer. Wait until you get a taste of the main course." Kayleigh gave him a naughty smirk that made his pulse race.

He slid his hands up her outer thigh and beneath her little black skirt.

No panties, either.

She flashed him another mischievous smile and pressed a slow, lingering kiss to his mouth before rising to her feet and walking toward his bedroom.

Parker shed his clothing, sheathed himself and had Kayleigh out of her skirt in the blink of an eye. He wrapped his arms around her waist, pulling their naked bodies together as he claimed her mouth in a greedy, impatient kiss that was fueled by his consuming desire for her.

He wanted her more than he'd ever wanted any woman. And he felt driven to bring her the deepest, most sensual pleasure possible.

Parker settled between her thighs and pressed a gentle kiss to the space between them. She shuddered and dug her heels into the mattress.

He placed another kiss there, relishing her taste: salty with a hint of sweetness. His eyes drifted closed as he parted her with his thumbs and dipped his tongue inside her.

Kayleigh rode his tongue, her soft whimpers escalating until she came completely undone. She shuddered as she called his name in a throaty, raw voice that sent shivers up his spine and made him want to do it all over again.

He made love to her. Tried to get his fill of her, knowing it would be the last time he'd have her in his bed.

Parker was awakened from a deep, satisfying sleep by the jangling of keys. He searched the room in the dark. A figure moved beside the bed.

"Kayleigh?" He sat up and turned on the bedside lamp. "You're leaving?"

"It's late. I should get home."

"Or you could stay."

"We both know you're not comfortable with that. It's fine. Really." Her tone indicated that it wasn't fine at all.

True. Normally he wasn't comfortable with that level of intimacy. But tonight he hungered for it. With her. "I'd really like it if you'd stay tonight…and tomorrow night."

She gave a small nod. "If you really want me to, I'll stay." She rummaged in her purse and then climbed back into bed. "But there's something I need to give you first."

"What's this?"

She shrugged. "Open it."

Parker put on his glasses and opened the box. It was a leather cuff bracelet with a steampunk-inspired skeleton watch with a clear dial that revealed its inner workings.

"Kayleigh, I don't know what to say." Parker traced the distressed brown leather and studied the exquisite workmanship of the piece. "This is—"

"It's not something you'd wear. Ever. I know." She smiled sheepishly. "And I honestly won't be insulted if you never wear it. But you wore that watch with the transparent face in New York, and I noticed that you read steampunk books. Something about that touched me. It reminded me of us as kids dressing up like pirates and space explorers. I wanted to make something for you that felt really personal and captured that little boy who still lives inside you. The boy who was once my best friend." Kayleigh dragged a finger beneath one eye. "Besides, I wanted you to know how much I appreciate everything you've done these past two months, and to leave you with something to remind you of our time together."

"Thank you, sweetheart…" He cradled her cheek and pressed a soft kiss to her lips. "It's extraordinary. I love it.

"That reminds me… I have something for you, too." Parker returned the watch to its box and set it on the bedside table. He got up and rummaged in his sock drawer.

"You've done so much already. I can't accept another gift."

"I think you'll make an exception for this one." Parker retrieved the box and removed the ring, which slipped from his fingers and rolled underneath the bed.

Parker cursed and dropped to his knees to search for it.

"Let me help you." Kayleigh swung her feet onto the floor.

"No, I've got it." Ring in hand, Parker knelt, preparing to stand. When he looked up at her gorgeous face, he was struck by how much he cared for her. How much he wished this was real. "I was going to give this to you right before we left on Monday. But it seems apropos that I give it to you now."

He held up the ring. "My friend came through. He

gave me a few options to choose from, but this one just felt like you."

Kayleigh pressed her fingertips to her mouth. "My God, Parker, it's beautiful. I can't believe I get to wear something this gorgeous, even if it's only for a week."

Parker gave her a pained smile and took her hand in his. He slid the intricate, rose-gold ring with a large, round center diamond and several swirled channels of smaller accent diamonds onto her finger.

"Kayleigh Louise Jemison, would you please agree to be my one and only fake fiancée?"

She laughed. "Yes, Parker Stephen Abbott, I promise *not* to marry you, but as your fake fiancée, I will happily wear this lovely ring."

Kayleigh cupped his cheek, leaned down and kissed him.

It was a sweet, tender kiss that reignited the deep passion he felt for her. He lay her back in bed and kissed her, made love to her, held her in his arms until she'd drifted off to sleep again.

But he lay awake for another hour, trying to hush the little voice deep inside his chest that kept growing louder. The one that kept telling him that what he felt for Kayleigh was real.

Seventeen

Kayleigh breathed in the salty air drifting off the Caribbean Sea as she exited the helicopter on the beautiful private island owned by the family of Kira Brennan's husband-to-be, Theodore Patrakis.

Parker offered her his hand as she stepped down. He looked concerned. "Having second thoughts about this?"

She was.

But after all the time and effort they'd put into preparing for it, there was no turning back now.

Kayleigh didn't answer his question. "Thank you." She tucked the clutch he'd given her in New York beneath her arm. "You're going to love Kira. She's the sweetest."

"She means a lot to you." Parker extended his elbow

and she slipped her arm through his. "So I look forward to meeting her."

His response left her speechless, as had many of the other sweet and thoughtful things he'd said or done in the past weeks.

They were escorted to a limousine shuttle that took them and a few other passengers to where they'd be staying. Within ten minutes, they had arrived in paradise.

"This place is amazing." Kayleigh kicked off her sandals and walked through their luxury seaside villa with folding glass doors, a hot tub, plunge pool and a deck overlooking the sea.

"It is," Parker agreed. "Looks like you're the one doing me a favor." He pulled Kayleigh into his arms and kissed her.

"Let me guess…you know just how to thank me." She couldn't help giggling when he nibbled on her ear.

"Nothing as trite as that." He kissed her neck. "Honestly, this is all I've been thinking about from the moment I saw you in that sundress this morning. I sat there on the plane, trying to work out the space and mechanics of joining the mile-high club."

"Parker Abbott, what has gotten into you?"

He cradled her face, his dark eyes staring intently at hers as he leaned in for another kiss. "You. And I'd like to return the favor."

Parker swept her up in his arms and carried her to the bedroom. He made love to her in the well-appointed luxury master suite with a wall of windows overlooking the sea and a small deck with seating.

Kayleigh would've been content spending the entire

week lying right there in Parker's arms. But they had to shower and change to make it to the welcome dinner later that night.

"Kayleigh! It's so good to see you!" Kira Brennan's baby blue eyes lit up. Her tousled blond beach waves dusted the fair, freckled skin of her shoulders.

"My God, Kira, look at you. You're gorgeous. You're going to make a beautiful bride." Eyes damp with tears, Kayleigh hugged her friend. Kira had grown into such a beautiful young woman. "Thank you so much for inviting us to be part of your wedding. The island is simply incredible."

Kira grinned up at the tall, handsome, dark-haired, olive-skinned man beside her. "This is my soon-to-be husband, Theodore Patrakis. Theo, this is Kayleigh and her fiancé. Parker Abbott, right?"

"Yes." Kayleigh's cheeks warmed as she glanced up at Parker. Her plan had seemed like a good one until she had to stand in front of Kira and tell her a lie, right to her face. Her hand trembled.

Parker slipped an arm around her waist and pulled her closer, a silent reminder that he was there for her. The tension in her shoulders eased instantly.

"Pleasure to meet you, Theo." Parker shook the man's hand. Then he shook Kira's. "I've heard so much about you from Kayleigh. It's a pleasure to finally meet you and an honor to be part of your wedding celebration."

Kira's eyes lit up and her smile was a silent *I like this guy.*

Kayleigh breathed a sigh of relief...until Kira asked her next question.

"So, I want to know everything. How did you two meet? What made you decide to get married? I want to hear it all." Kira squeezed Kayleigh's hand.

Kayleigh turned to glance at Parker, but he was focused on Kira.

"I've known Kayleigh since we were kids. I didn't know it then, but I fell in love with her when I was maybe nine years old. She was beautiful and fierce and uniquely her own person. Confident in her own skin, regardless of what anyone else said or did. I admired those qualities even then." Parker turned to her. His deep, genuine smile and the dreamy look in his dark eyes made her heart flutter.

"Parker was brilliant, even when we were kids. Maybe too much for his own good." Kayleigh shifted her gaze back to Kira. "We both made some mistakes and our friendship ended badly. But in recent months, we decided to renew our friendship. Things just progressed from there."

"And let me see the ring." Kira held Kayleigh's hand and admired the unique ring that Parker had given her just a few days earlier. "Kayleigh, it's beautiful. And it's perfect for you. Did you pick it out yourself?"

"No." Kayleigh smiled at Parker. "Parker did that on his own. He knows me even better than I thought."

"My God, you're both just so cute and so in love. I'm thrilled for you, Kayleigh. I really am. You deserve to be happy." Kira leaned in and kissed her cheek. "Theo and I need to make the rounds, but we'll catch up more later."

Kira slipped her hand in Theo's as they went over to greet the other guests.

"Relax. You did just fine." Parker's soothing deep voice and warm breath on Kayleigh's ear calmed her.

She released a heavy sigh and nodded, glancing up at him. "Thank you for being here, Parker. I honestly don't think I could've done this with anyone else."

Parker's cheeks flushed. He leaned in and gave her a quick kiss on the lips. "I'm glad I'm here, too."

"Kayleigh, so glad you could make it." Colleen Brennan approached with a flute of champagne in her hand. Her dark hair was a perfect contrast to the icy blue eyes that suited her so well. At nearly sixty she was still stunningly beautiful, and the crisp white linen dress she wore complemented her figure. "And this handsome gentleman must be your fiancé, Parker Abbott. Looks like you found your perfect match."

Parker's back tensed beneath Kayleigh's arm and his expression hardened. She tightened her grip around his waist, a silent plea for him not to make a scene with the bride's mother.

"I have," Kayleigh said simply. "And I couldn't be happier."

They'd stayed out late and drunk far too much. Parker slept in the next morning, but Kayleigh needed to burn off some of the nervous energy that left her lying awake most of the night while Parker slept soundly.

She'd met the entire wedding party and encountered many of Aidan and Kira's aunts, uncles and cousins again at last night's dinner. The one person she hadn't seen was Aidan. She wouldn't allow herself to ask about him, but she'd found herself glancing around the room and expecting every new person who walked through the door to be him.

"Aidan won't arrive until tomorrow," Kira had whispered in her ear when she joined Kayleigh at the dessert buffet.

"I wasn't looking for Aidan," she'd said quickly as she debated over the tiramisu and crème brûlée.

"It's okay, Kayleigh. It's understandable that you'd both be nervous about seeing each other again after all this time. But there's something I should confess. I invited you to be in my wedding for all of the reasons I told you before. But I had another reason for inviting you. I—"

"What looks good for dessert, ladies?" Parker had appeared beside them suddenly.

"Everything. I've tried them all." Kira had flashed her broad smile and then excused herself to join Theo and his family.

There hadn't been another opportunity to speak to Kira alone, and all night Kayleigh couldn't help wondering what other motive Kira had for making her a part of her wedding.

Since Parker was sound asleep, Kayleigh slipped out of bed and put on shorts, a tank top and running shoes. She headed out to the beach for a long run and didn't stop until she got to the end of the stretch of white sand. Then she turned around and jogged back to their villa.

"Kayleigh Jemison. My God, how long has it been?" Aidan Brennan called as she reached the top of the stairs that led up from the beach.

He'd grown his red hair out past his ears, and his beard was longer than she'd ever seen it. There were lines around his vibrant blue eyes.

"It's been a long time, Aidan." Kayleigh turned to face him as he approached. "Seven years, at least."

The day before, she'd been picture perfect. But of course she would run into Aidan while she was drenched with perspiration, her hair was pulled up in a messy top-knot and she smelled like sweat and sand.

"It's been too long." He pulled her into a hug, his ginger beard scraping her shoulder. Aidan released her and sighed as he took a step back and shoved his hands in his pockets. "I hear you're engaged now."

"I am." She dropped her gaze from his, then forced a smile. "And I hear you're an old married man with two beautiful children."

"I am the father of two handsome boys." Aidan frowned and ran a hand through his longish hair, which rustled with the gentle breeze and covered one eye. "But I've been divorced for the past two years. The boys live in Ireland with their mother and her new beau. I try to see them as often as I can…which is why I didn't arrive until today. I'd hoped to bring them back with me, but my ex-wife wouldn't permit it. She's afraid if I bring the boys stateside, I won't bring them back."

"Aidan, I'm sorry. I didn't realize—"

He waved a hand. "You couldn't have known."

Kayleigh breathed a sigh of relief. She hadn't wanted to hurt Aidan then, and she surely didn't want to hurt him now. They stood together in awkward silence. Neither of them seemed to know what to say.

"Aidan, if you don't mind me asking, what happened between you two? By all accounts, you were a perfect pair."

"On the surface, I s'pose you're right. But once we had the boys and I was consumed by my growing role in our family business…things changed. After that initial fiery passion died down, there just wasn't enough to sustain the relationship." He lowered his voice. "She and I were never as well-suited as you and I were."

Kayleigh's cheeks stung.

Was this what Kira was trying to tell her? That Aidan was single again and she'd wanted to give them a second chance?

Her chest ached and her head suddenly felt light. Fate had conspired to give her and Aidan a second chance at love, and she'd countered it with a fake-fiancé scheme.

Maybe the day Kira had made that call, she would've jumped at the chance to try again with Aidan. To tell him the truth about what his mother had done. But the past three months with Parker had changed everything.

She'd loved Aidan very much back then, but that was ancient history. She'd developed deep feelings for Parker. And after the wedding was over, she planned to tell him just that.

"I'd invite you in for a cup of coffee, but my fiancé is still asleep. I don't want to wake him."

Kayleigh tucked a loose strand of hair behind her ear. "But I guess I'll see you at lunch later."

He gave her a sad smile. "Count on it."

Kayleigh heaved a sigh as Aidan walked away. Then she turned up the path toward the villa she shared with Parker.

Eighteen

Parker stared out the window of the villa at Kayleigh, who was obviously distressed about her interaction with her ex. He'd been tempted to rush out to her side and finally meet the esteemed Aidan Brennan. But it didn't seem prudent to admit that he'd been anxiously awaiting her return like some sad little puppy and eavesdropping on the entire conversation.

He divided a split of champagne between two flutes and then poured a little freshly squeezed orange juice in both.

"Hey." Kayleigh seemed surprised to find him up and among the living after the way he'd crashed last night.

"Good morning." He handed her a mimosa.

Kayleigh looked at the open bottle of champagne on the bar. "It's a little early to start drinking, isn't it?"

"Thought you might need it after running into your ex."

"You heard that, huh?" She sipped the mimosa.

"I just happened to be near the window and heard him call your name." So much for keeping his eaves-dropping to himself. "He seems like a nice enough guy."

"I never said he wasn't." Her tone was sharp.

He'd evidently irritated Kayleigh, though he wasn't sure why. It seemed best to move on to a different topic.

"You're probably hungry after your run. I'll order breakfast whenever you're ready." He walked toward the patio.

"Parker, look, I'm sorry." Kayleigh set down her glass. "I guess I'm just feeling… I don't know what I'm feeling." She settled onto the barstool.

"Maybe you're wondering if you've thwarted fate by setting up this charade? Or if Aidan might've been your best shot at happiness?" Parker asked tentatively, hoping Kayleigh would deny it.

She shrugged instead. "Something like that. Mostly I regret not telling Aidan the truth about his precious mother. It's like you said—I took away his choice be-cause I was afraid he wouldn't choose me."

"I can understand why you might have some re-grets." He certainly did. Why hadn't he kept his ob-servations to himself?

"I'm sorry if I was short with you earlier. Seeing Aidan again after all these years was more intense than I thought it would be." Kayleigh downed the remainder of her mimosa and stood. "Why don't you go ahead and order breakfast? I'm gonna hit the shower. I promise to be in a much better mood when I get out." She forced a smile and pressed a quick kiss to his cheek before ducking into the bedroom.

Parker sank onto the sofa and sighed, his gaze still fixed on the door she'd just closed behind her.

During the past few weeks, he'd discovered that beneath the mangled wreckage of his and Kayleigh's friendship lay strong feelings that ran true and deep.

But as strongly as he felt for her, it seemed she didn't feel the same. Hearing her regrets about Aidan was like a cannon ball being launched into his chest.

It was Aidan Brennan she truly wanted. Parker had only been a convenient substitute.

He finished his mimosa and set the glass down hard on a nearby table. He wanted to be with Kayleigh. Not as a sham relationship or just for sex. He wanted it to be genuine. Because he loved her.

He'd picked one hell of a time to have that realization.

Parker paced the floor. The memories of that day in middle school were still as fresh as the day they'd happened. He hadn't initially set out to make fun of Kayleigh's father. But he'd mentioned a fact about the man in passing and several of his popular classmates laughed hysterically. The kids who didn't normally give him and Kayleigh the time of day.

They'd wanted to hear more about her father's escapades, so he'd obliged. For once, he was the one telling the joke, rather than the joke being on him.

But he hadn't had long to relish his status with the popular kids. He could still see the heartbreak in Kayleigh's eyes and the tears staining her cheeks when she'd overheard him telling an especially embarrassing story about her father and the chorus of laughter that rang out in that hallway.

He'd selfishly ruined their relationship by putting his best interest ahead of their friendship, and he'd lost her. Now that they'd rekindled that friendship, he couldn't risk losing it again. Even if it meant sacrificing his desire for something more with her. Because more than anything, he wanted Kayleigh to finally have some of the happiness that had eluded her for most of her life.

If Kayleigh wanted a life with Aidan Brennan, he loved her enough to want that for her, too.

But Aidan's belief that he and Kayleigh were engaged had ruined the prospect of the two of them finding their way back to each other.

It was a monumental dilemma, but Parker would do whatever it took for her to be happy.

Kayleigh stood on the terrace overlooking the Caribbean, watching the waves crash against the shore. They'd had another lovely dinner, and the evening was winding down.

Parker had been incredibly supportive. He'd gone out of his way to be personable with Kira, Theo and their wedding guests. He'd even taken a liking to Aidan. She'd initially found it unsettling. But Aidan seemed grateful for the break from his overprotective mother and prying aunts and cousins.

"Hey, you. What are you doing out here all by yourself?" Kira slipped her arm through Kayleigh's and laid her head on her shoulder.

"Just enjoying the view." Kayleigh leaned her head against Kira's. "Why aren't you in there with your incredibly handsome husband-to-be?"

Kira sighed softly. "I just needed a little break, I guess. I swear, if one more of our relatives asks when we're going to start having babies, I'm going to scream." Kira lifted her head and turned to Kayleigh. "Is it terrible that I don't want kids right away? That I'd like to bask in being the center of Theo's attention for now?"

"Of course not." Kayleigh turned to Kira and squeezed her hand. "And don't let anyone tell you differently. It's up to you and Theo to decide what you want. Everyone else can take a flying leap."

"Thank you." Kira nodded and turned to look at the water, too. They were both quiet for a moment before she spoke again. "So, you've probably figured out the other reason I wanted you to be here."

"Aidan." Kayleigh said his name softly as she turned to her friend. "You were trying to fix what your mother had done."

"He's never stopped regretting the day he stood by and let you walk away without a fight. I thought that once you saw each other…" Kira sighed heavily. "I know what you're thinking."

"How very *Parent Trap* of you?"

"Something like that," Kira said.

"But you knew that I was bringing my fiancé." Kayleigh shoved Kira lightly with her shoulder.

"Honestly? I figured he was some random guy you

were bringing to make my brother jealous." Kira shook her head. "But then I met him and got to see you two together. There's no mistaking that look in both of your eyes. He's obviously in love with you, and you love him, too. So despite my little scheme backfiring, I'm really happy for you, Kayleigh."

Kira leaned in and kissed her cheek. "I'd better get back to the party before—"

"Kira! Kira, darling, what are you doing out here?" Colleen Brennan peeked out of the French doors that led to the terrace. Her thin lips pressed into a harsh line and her nostrils flared.

Kira exchanged a look with Kayleigh, then sighed. "Coming, Mother."

Kayleigh sat in a nearby seat, her heart racing as Kira's words turned over in her head.

He's obviously in love with you, and you love him, too.

Kayleigh swallowed hard and tears stung her eyes. Her feelings for Parker had been building so gradually over the past few months. There'd been a growing affection between them for sure, and a passion that sent tingles up her spine whenever she thought of him. But love?

She'd convinced herself that Parker Abbott wasn't capable of truly loving anyone whose last name wasn't Abbott from birth. Even then, she'd suspected he only tolerated them. But seeing the interactions between Parker and his family up close...there was no doubt about the love between them. And he'd gone out of his way to fulfill his duties as her fake fiancé. She couldn't have asked for anything more.

Was it because he honestly did feel something for her?

"Kayleigh, there you are." Parker joined her on the terrace and sat beside her. "I have some work to do tonight, so I'm going to head back to the villa. But Aidan promised to see you back safely."

"If you need to leave, I'll come with you." She started to get up.

Parker halted her with a hand pressed firmly to her arm. "Don't feel you need to leave on my account. Besides, I could use the alone time to get some work done."

"Oh. Sure." She tried her hardest not to sound as hurt as she felt. It wasn't just that night. Parker's mood had changed. The first day and night they'd spent there on the island, they'd made love every chance they got. But in the past couple of nights, he seemed to be slowly pulling away…physically and emotionally. Her gaze met his. "Parker, have I done something to upset you?"

"No, of course not." He kissed the back of her hand and gave her what felt like a forced smile. "It's nothing like that."

"Then it is something." She echoed his words to her that day at the cabin.

"I've got things to do—that's all. Will you be all right?"

She nodded in silence and he leaned in and kissed her cheek.

As she watched him walk away, it was clear that there was more to the story. But he obviously didn't trust her enough to share. Just as he hadn't been willing to share with her exactly why he'd wanted to purchase her building and what their plans for it were.

Kayleigh turned back to stare out onto the water. Kira was only half right. She had fallen for Parker, but he clearly didn't feel the same way about her.

Parker paced on the terrace, his palms damp and his pulse jumping in his temple. The wedding party was winding down with the rehearsal, and the rehearsal dinner would start soon. Tonight was the night.

It's now or never, Park.

His eyes drifted closed and he sighed heavily. He'd spent the week getting to know Aidan Brennan. He needed to be sure that he was truly worthy of Kayleigh.

By all accounts, Aidan was a good and decent man. Despite the unfortunate circumstances with his ex-wife, he was doing his best to remain in the lives of his children. And he'd proven himself to be a savvy businessman, expanding the family's company's reach considerably since he'd taken the reins over from his father, who'd died many years before.

Parker had watched Aidan's interaction with Kayleigh. He still adored her. Even Parker could see that. Kayleigh obviously still cared deeply for Aidan, too.

He reflected on the pain and loneliness in Kayleigh's voice and the hurt in her eyes after she'd first encountered Aidan. It was a look he'd never forget. He'd been the cause of that pain before. In a way, he was the cause of it now.

He loved Kayleigh and he wanted her to be happy.

For the briefest moment, he'd believed she could be happy with him. But the truth was that the man he'd been with her these past three months wasn't the person he'd been most of his life.

He wasn't fun-loving and spontaneous. Wasn't outdoorsy or a dancer. Wasn't adored by pets or small kids. He wasn't the kind of man who cuddled and spent the night or who spent his days daydreaming about anyone.

But for her, he had been.

Shouldn't that have set off alarm bells in his head? They both deserved to be with someone who loved them just the way they were. Not someone who'd force them to become someone else.

Parker sighed.

Kayleigh hadn't pressured him to be someone else. She'd simply introduced him to life outside of his comfort zone. And as much as he hated to admit it, he'd found enjoyment in activities he'd never thought he would. Just as she seemed to appreciate the new, more organized processes he'd introduced her to when he'd helped her organize her storeroom cabinet and switch to a user-friendly accounting software she'd actually use.

Maybe each of them simply made the other better.

"Parker." Aidan had stepped out onto the balcony. "Kayleigh asked me to tell you that she and the other bridesmaids are in a last-minute meeting with my sister. They'll return before dinner."

Parker stared at the man, his heart racing.

"Everything okay? You don't look well." Aidan came closer.

"I'm fine. I just wondered if we could talk for a minute." He would never get a more ideal moment than right now.

"Sure." Aidan shrugged. He leaned against the railing. "You've been quiet today. Is something wrong?"

"When we first met, you said that I was lucky to be with Kayleigh, and that you envied our happiness." Parker walked over and stood beside Aidan. "Was that a platitude, or were you being sincere?"

Aidan cocked his head and folded his arms over his chest. "I'm not sure what you're getting at or that I like the direction of this conversation."

"I understand, but I really need to know how you feel about Kayleigh. She's an incredible woman and she deserves to be happy. I'll do whatever I have to do to make that happen."

"Whoa!" Aidan held up his hands as he backed away. "I don't know what you and Kayleigh are into, but—"

"Relax, man. What I'm trying to say is that I think Kayleigh regrets walking away from you, too. That given the chance to do it again…maybe she'd have stayed and fought for you."

"She's your fiancée, and she seems quite taken with you. So why are you telling me all of this?"

Once he crossed this line, he couldn't go back. There was no way to put the genie back into the bottle. Most important, he'd be risking the plans they'd worked so hard on.

"Kayleigh isn't my fiancée," he said quietly.

"What do you mean?" Aidan's expression morphed

from confusion to anger. "What kind of game are you two running?"

"Let me explain." Parker sighed. "Kayleigh didn't want to show up here alone and face you with your perfect little family. She asked me to pose as her fiancé."

"You lied to my sister and everyone here." Aidan's fists were clenched at his side.

"And I'm sorry, but there was no nefarious plot. It was simply a matter of Kayleigh wanting to keep her pride." Parker sank onto a chair and tapped a finger on the patio table. "She didn't want you to know that she was still very much alone."

Aidan heaved a sigh and sat, too. Neither of them spoke for several seconds. Finally he asked, "And exactly what do you expect me to do with this information?"

Parker's chest tightened. He stared down at his hands, folded in his lap, his shoulders drooping forward. The world seemed to be spinning.

"That depends on how you feel about her. If you love her still and you're ready to give her another chance, then tell her how you really feel. If not, I'd beg you not to reveal this conversation to her or anyone. We can all just go back to the way things were."

Everything inside him hoped like hell that Aidan would choose the latter. That he'd get up and walk away, pretending as if they'd never had this conversation.

"Do you really believe she wants to try again?" Aidan asked.

Parker forced a bitter smile, his lips pressed together

tightly as he collapsed against the back of the chair and swallowed hard. "I think she's been wondering if she blew a second chance for you two by bringing me here."

Aidan nodded his head. He stood, extending a hand to Parker. "Thank you for telling me this. It couldn't have been an easy decision. You obviously care a lot about her."

"I do." Parker shook the man's hand as he rose to his feet. "So don't fuck this up."

"I won't, and I won't mention this to my sister or mother. But please, don't tell Kayleigh that you told me."

Parker nodded without speaking and shoved his hands in his pocket as he watched Aidan walk away with a renewed energy to his gait.

He'd done it. Risked the deal. Risked losing her friendship again. Risked any shot of pulling ahead of Blake as the next CEO. But he couldn't stand idly by and do nothing, knowing he'd had a chance to give her everything she deserved.

He walked inside to the bar and ordered a glass of King's Finest bourbon, neat.

Nineteen

Kayleigh was exhausted. As beautiful as the wedding had been, it felt like the longest day ever. It had begun with a bridesmaids' breakfast, and then there was all of the primping. Manicures and pedicures. Getting their hair and makeup done.

Suddenly she remembered why she was so low-maintenance. She had neither the time nor inclination for all of the upkeep required for her to look like this every single day. But for this one magical day, she'd looked perfect. And the expression on Parker's face when their eyes met as she took her turn walking down the aisle was priceless.

Kayleigh smoothed down the front of her chiffon bridesmaid's dress with the high-low hem. She loved the vintage mauve color Kira had chosen. The formal length of the back of the dress created a nice visual as each of the bridesmaids walked down the aisle, while the shorter length of the front of the dress allowed her to move about freely. She'd ditched the strappy nude stilettos after the bridal party's intricately choreographed dance they'd spent three days learning.

Now all she really wanted to do was spend the rest of the night with Parker. Something she hadn't done much of over the past few days.

"Hey, handsome." Kayleigh snuck up behind Parker, seated at his table, and wrapped her arms around his shoulders. She pressed a kiss to his cheek. "Care to dance?"

His expression was an odd mix of deep affection and abject sadness that startled her.

"Is everything okay? Did something happen back home?"

"Everything is fine." He kissed her hand softly. "And yes, I'd love to dance with you."

Parker took her hand and followed her to the dance floor. Kayleigh wrapped her arms around him and they moved to the music. The muscles in his back were tense and he barely spoke.

Kayleigh stared up at him. "Parker, are you sure everything is all right?"

He nodded, but his sad smile barely turned up the corners of his mouth. "You look incredible, Kayleigh. I couldn't take my eyes off you."

Some of the tension in her shoulders eased. "Really?"

"Absolutely." His smile seemed more genuine. "Kira was beautiful, but you were the star of the show for me."

"You look pretty handsome yourself." A full grin spread across her face. She stared up at him again as she ran her fingers beneath the lapels of his cream-colored suit. It was the perfect shade for an outdoor wedding in the Caribbean. "I'm sorry we haven't had much time to spend together the last few days."

"You came here to help Kira and Theo celebrate their big day. Besides, I had plenty to keep me busy."

"Remember when we had to dance together at Blake and Savannah's wedding? How different things were between us?" Kayleigh sighed. "I wish things could've been like this then."

"So do I."

Kayleigh wished she could lay her head on his chest, the way she had when they'd danced by the pool at the cabin in the mountains. But her makeup would ruin his white linen shirt.

"Parker, I can't thank you enough for doing this. All of it. You've been so accommodating and nothing short of amazing. You're going to make an awesome fiancé someday." She forced a smile, her eyes searching his.

"Thanks." He quickly shifted his gaze from hers. "So will you. As for this trip, I think I'm the one who owes you. I hadn't been on an honest-to-goodness vacation in so long. And this was one hell of a trip. I won't forget it or any of the incredible moments that proceeded it."

"You're wearing the watch." She touched the leather band and smiled. "You didn't have to, you know. But I'm glad you did."

The music ended and they played a faster-paced

song. Kayleigh's eyes met his and she braced his arms, holding him in place. "You know what I'd really like to do right now? I'd like to go back to our villa and…" She lifted onto her toes and whispered the rest in his ear.

His cheeks and forehead turned bright red as his eyes searched hers. "You're not making this easy for me, Kayleigh."

"I thought you enjoyed a challenge." Kayleigh grinned.

It was a beautiful night as they danced beneath the stars. But all she wanted now was to go back to their villa and spend their remaining hours in paradise making love and lying in each other's arms. And before they boarded the plane, she would find the courage to tell him the truth. Somewhere along the way, she'd fallen in love with him.

Parker took Kayleigh's hand and led her to the pier overlooking the water, away from where the partygoers danced.

Kayleigh's heart raced. When they stopped, she studied his expression. He was distressed. So clearly, whatever news he intended to deliver wasn't going to be good.

"Oh, God. It's that bad, huh?" Kayleigh wrapped her arms around herself, suddenly chilled by the cool breeze blowing off the sea. "So it isn't my imagination. You've been intentionally distant for the past few days."

"Kayleigh, I—"

"I feel like I should've had a drink to prepare me for this little talk." She laughed bitterly.

"We just toasted with champagne." Parker leaned against the railing.

"I was thinking of something a little stronger…like a dirty martini. Would you mind?" She needed the space and a few minutes to clear her head as much as she wanted that martini.

"Don't go anywhere. We need to talk."

Kayleigh nodded without looking at Parker. Tears stung her eyes as she stared out onto the water.

A few minutes later, she felt arms slip around her waist and lips nuzzle the back of her neck. Her eyes, which had drifted closed momentarily, quickly widened when she felt the scrape of a thick beard on her skin and recognized the distinctive cologne.

She whirled around to face Aidan. "What in the hell are you doing?"

His blue eyes danced and there was a mischievous smile on his face. He ran his fingers through his hair. "Kissing your neck, which if memory serves me, is something you've always favored."

Kayleigh folded her arms. "Did you suddenly forget that I'm engaged to someone else?"

His smirk deepened and the amusement in his eyes was unmistakable. Aidan shoved his hands into the pockets of the beige suit the groom and his grooms-men wore for the ceremony.

Her heart suddenly pounded in her chest and the entire world seemed to be spinning faster and faster. A knot tightened in her gut.

"You know, don't you?"

Aidan's smile turned into a full-fledged grin as he cradled her cheek and leaned in to kiss her.

Kayleigh shoved her hands against his chest and stepped backward. "How did you find out? Let me guess, your mother had someone look into me. That's low, even for Colleen."

"No, why would you think my mother was involved?" Aidan wasn't smiling anymore. "And what do you mean by it being low, even for her?"

"If your mother didn't tell you, then how did you know?"

"Your 'fiancé' told me the truth." He used air quotes.

"Wait… Parker told you." Kayleigh felt a sharp pain in her chest and tears stung her eyes. "No." She shook her head. "Parker wouldn't." She uttered the words under her breath, more to herself than to Aidan.

Maybe Parker didn't care about the crushing humiliation of such a revelation, but what he did care about was King's Finest. And that her building was an important part of the company's future expansion. So Parker wouldn't have violated their agreement. He wouldn't have risked losing the very thing he'd gone through all of this to obtain.

"He did."

"Why?" Her voice cracked, even as she tried to keep her composure.

Aidan's expression softened, all of the teasing gone. He took her hands in his and met her watery gaze. "Because I still love you, Kayleigh. And because you obviously still have feelings for me. Why else would you go to such elaborate lengths to make me jealous?"

"You think I did this because I wanted to make you jealous?" Her tone grew more indignant and the corners of her eyes were wet with tears.

"Didn't you?"

"No." She jerked her hands from his grip and stepped farther away. "Maybe my reasons for it were silly or even a little petty, but I did *not* do this to make you jealous. I thought you were still married."

"Then if making me jealous wasn't your aim, what was it? Why would you manufacture a fiancé and bring him all the way here to my sister's wedding?"

Kayleigh angrily wiped at her eyes with her knuckle. "I didn't want to show up here alone and watch you and your runway-model wife playing with your two beautiful little boys while I'm still—"

"Alone?" Aidan sighed, placing a tentative hand on her arm. "Kayleigh, there's nothing wrong with being alone. I wouldn't have thought any less of you because of it, whether I was still married or not."

"Maybe you wouldn't, but your mother certainly would. I just couldn't bear the thought of proving her right."

"About?"

"About me not being a suitable wife for her precious son." She raised her eyes to his again. "Or anyone, for that matter." Her last words were practically whispered.

"Are you saying that you walking away back then had something to do with my mother?"

It was his sister's wedding, and it had been such a lovely event. She hadn't told Aidan or Kira about her conversation with Colleen Brennan that day. Nor did she want to talk about it now.

What would be the point?

"Look, Aidan, none of that matters anymore. Yes, when I first learned that you were no longer married, I wondered if I'd screwed up a second chance for us." Kayleigh dabbed at her eyes, which were brimming with hot tears. "But spending this week with your family…it reminded me of all the reasons that walking away then…and now…is the right thing to do. I'm sorry."

Kayleigh lifted onto her toes and placed a soft kiss on Aidan's whiskered cheek.

He held her there. His rough beard scraped the side of her face and his lips brushed her ear as he whispered into it. "I didn't fight for you then. I was devastated by your rejection and I was furious that you chose to just walk away. I didn't ask the right questions then. So I'm asking you right now. Is there anything I can do to make you reconsider?"

Kayleigh pulled away enough to look into his blue eyes. Her chest ached for the pain she saw there, knowing she'd been at least partially responsible for it. She slowly shook her head, her expression a tortured apology.

"Why not, sweetheart?" His sincere, determined gaze almost broke her heart. Aidan didn't deserve any of this.

"Because…I love someone else." She took a step away when he finally released her arm. "And because as wonderful as this week has been, it's also been a reminder that this isn't the life or the family I want. I love my life in Magnolia Lake. Maybe I don't have family or a fiancé there, but I have amazing friends and a really good life and future. I'm not ready to give any of that up, Aidan. I'm sorry."

"Okay." He shrugged, running a hand through his hair again. "At least I tried, right?"

"And I thank you for caring enough to." Kayleigh gave him a faint smile. "Please, don't tell Kira or your mother. I'd be mortified. Besides, it's been such a marvelous week, I don't want to ruin it for her. Not even a little."

Aidan nodded. "I promise."

"Thank you. Please make my apologies to Kira and Theo, but I'm not feeling well. I'm going back to my villa to lie down." She turned to walk away, but then glanced back over her shoulder. "It was good seeing you again, Aidan."

Kayleigh hurried back to her villa as quickly as she could, tears streaming down her face. She was furious with Parker for betraying her trust again, just as he had more than two decades ago. But most of all, she was disappointed in herself for falling for a man who clearly didn't want or deserve her.

Twenty

Parker settled into a chair in their villa, his elbows on his knees and his forehead cradled in his palm. His heartbeat had been elevated by his hurried retreat back to the villa, but mostly because of seeing Kayleigh and Aidan in a tight embrace as the man whispered something in her ear.

Parker shut his eyes, replaying the evening in his mind. He wasn't sure what had been sexier. The way Kayleigh had looked in that dress or the mind-blowingly sensual thing she had whispered in his ear, which evoked a visual he simply couldn't get out of his head now, even if he tried. Sadly, they wouldn't get to act it out.

More important, he'd never have her in his life or his bed again. She'd probably move to Atlanta to be with Aidan. Or maybe they'd even move to Ireland to be closer to his children. Either way, the most Parker could hope was that the friendship they'd slowly resurrected, brick by painstaking brick, would endure.

He heard the screen door slam suddenly and jumped to his feet. It was Kayleigh. She was furious. Her eyes were red and her face was streaked with tears.

"How could you do this to me again? Why would you do it? Were you that desperate to be rid of me? Or was this all just a big joke to you?" Her bare feet slapped against the tile floor as she stalked toward him.

His act of selflessness obviously hadn't gone to plan. She knew he'd told Aidan the truth and she was furious.

"Kayleigh, how could you think that, even for a moment, I wanted to hurt you?"

"Because you just fucking did. *Again*. And I let you because I was stupid enough to think…" Kayleigh shook her head, jaw trembling. "It doesn't matter what I thought. I was wrong. But what I don't understand is why you would go through ten weeks of this—" she gestured between them "—and then jeopardize our deal by doing the one thing I asked you not to do?"

It was a fair question. One he struggled to answer.

"You know what? Forget it. *Why* doesn't even matter." Kayleigh walked out onto the wraparound deck and stood against the railing that overlooked the beach and the waters of the sea beyond it.

"Kayleigh, let me explain." Parker followed her outside. She stood there in her bare feet, the long train of her dusty-mauve dress billowing behind her.

When he grasped her arm, she turned around, like she was five seconds away from swinging on him.

Her chest heaved, likely as much from her fury as from the exertion of trying to distance herself from him.

"Don't touch me." She yanked her hand free. Her eyes filled with fresh tears. "I can't believe I trusted you again. That I was stupid enough to believe we'd actually become friends again at the very least. Do you really hate me this much, Parker? Was this your grand plan all along? To wait until we got here so that you could utterly humiliate me?"

"I could never hate you, Kayleigh, and I didn't do this to hurt you. I swear."

"Even if you got some kind of sick enjoyment out of doing this to me again, I thought you were disciplined enough not to blow up our deal and let your family down." Kayleigh swiped the backs of her fingers beneath her eyes. "What was it? Did I get too clingy? Were you afraid that I wanted more with you?"

"No, of course not, sweetheart. I've enjoyed every single moment we spent together over the past three months."

"Then why, for God's sake, would you do this?"

"Because I hated seeing how much it hurt you that things worked out between you and Aidan the way they did. You seemed to genuinely want a second chance with him. I could never have forgiven myself if I'd stood in the way of you *finally* being happy. I thought that if I told Aidan the truth—"

"That you could just pass me on to him because we were done? I'm not a baton, Parker." Her eyes blazed with anger and her voice dripped with disdain. "You don't get to decide who I love or what I do. That's *my* choice."

Parker stammered, his heart hammering against his breastbone.

"It was stupid of me to think I could make this work." She sniffled, looking out at the water. "You said you didn't want to do this. That you *couldn't* do it. I just wouldn't listen."

"I'm so sorry if I hurt you. That honestly wasn't my intention. I thought you *wanted* to be with Aidan."

Her eyes widened with indignation and her nostrils flared. She shook her head as if discussing the matter with him any further was pointless. "Go away, Parker. Just leave me alone, please."

She stalked into the bedroom and slammed the door behind her.

Parker's gut burned and his chest ached. He'd tried to give Kayleigh what he thought she wanted. Even though it was the one thing in the world that made him feel like his heart had been ripped in two.

Because he loved Kayleigh Jemison, and he couldn't imagine going back to life without her.

Kayleigh wanted to get out of the dress and makeup and maybe go for a run on the beach. Clear her head and pull herself together.

In the three months that she had been seeing Parker, she'd turned into a hot mess. And she hated herself for it. Before now, the only emotion she'd voluntarily let others see was anger. Everything else she'd kept concealed neatly below the surface. Out of sight, where they couldn't use those weaknesses against her. It was a neat trick she'd learned in middle school and had used ever since.

Concealing those painful emotions from others had kept her from feeling vulnerable. But it had isolated her, too. That had changed when she allowed Savannah in. And over the past few months, she'd let Parker in.

A few weeks ago, she'd seen the beauty of allowing someone else in and permitting them to see those vulnerabilities. But now she was reminded of the importance of choosing more wisely who to let in.

Kayleigh heaved a sigh and stood in front of the full-length mirror. She reached over her shoulder to unzip the back of her dress. Then she reached behind her to tug it down the rest of the way.

"Let me." Parker was suddenly there, standing behind her as he stared at her reflection in the mirror. "Please."

Kayleigh sighed, nodding as she dropped her gaze from his.

Parker unzipped the dress, then stepped away.

She allowed the fabric to pool around her on the floor, then tossed it onto the bed before going into the bathroom and removing her makeup.

Kayleigh stared into the mirror of the elegant bathroom, scrubbing the makeup from her skin as Parker leaned against the doorway in silence.

She met his gaze in the mirror. "What is it, Parker? Haven't you done enough?"

"I need to tell you how sorry I am that I hurt you. I was a little jerk when we were kids. Maybe I still am. But then and now, I didn't deliberately try to hurt you. My motives back then were selfish. But I swear to you that what

I did today was the most selfless thing I've ever done. And I did it because I thought that's what you wanted."

"To be embarrassed?"

"To be loved and cherished and treated like the phenomenal woman you are." His voice grew faint and he took another deep breath. "I honestly just wanted you to have everything and to be happy, and if I can't be the man who gives that to you... I wanted to see you with someone who will."

"That's exactly what I'm talking about, Parker. I know you think it's your job to fix everything, but you don't get to decide who... Wait..." Kayleigh lowered the finger she'd been emphatically jabbing in the air. She tilted her head to one side as she studied him. "Are you saying that *you* want to be the one who makes me happy?"

"Not very well, I'm guessing. But yes, Kayleigh." Parker stepped closer, cradling her face in his hands. "I want to be the only man who truly makes you smile. I want to be the guy you walk Cricket with at night. The one you go riding and camping with. The guy you volunteer beside at the youth center each month. The one you go skinny-dipping with in the middle of the night." Parker traced her cheekbone with his thumb. "I want to be the only man you make love to."

Kayleigh closed her eyes and leaned into his touch as tears spilled down her cheeks. She sniffled, finally opening them. A wide smile spread across her face. "I want that, too, Parker. But I need to know I can trust you. That you won't betray my confidence for *any* reason."

He nodded. "I promise. I love you, Kayleigh. I've adored you since we were kids. And I never stopped thinking of you and wanting you back in my life. I've never felt this way about anyone before. So forgive me for screwing up."

"You love me?" Her voice trembled as she stared into his dark eyes, which were filled with emotion.

The corner of his mouth curved in a smile. "Very much. But it's more than that. I need you, Kayleigh. When I saw Aidan holding you in his arms, I felt physical pain. Like an elephant was standing on my chest and my lungs were about to collapse. If someone had said that to me a few months ago, I would've accused them of being melodramatic. But being heartbroken is a real thing because I felt every ounce of that pain."

"So did I when..." Kayleigh couldn't finish the words. She didn't want to be reminded of the pain she'd felt in that moment. She pressed a gentle kiss to his lips. "I love you, too, Parker."

Parker took Kayleigh in his arms and kissed her again. He needed to feel the warmth and comfort of her body. To show her exactly how much he needed her in his life. That he'd never hurt her again.

He stripped her of her pink lace panties and bra and laid her on the bed beneath him as he claimed her mouth in a heated kiss that made his body ache to be inside of hers.

Kayleigh ground her hips against his as she tugged his shirt from his waistband and helped him remove it and his linen pants.

Parker grazed one firm nipple with the backs of his fingers until it strained against his touch as he kissed her. He closed his eager mouth over the beaded tip and sucked roughly. She gasped and arched her back.

His eyes drifted closed as ripples of need rolled down his spine in response to her soft whimpers. His pulse raced and body vibrated with his desire to be buried inside of her, but he needed to take his time. Focus on pleasuring every inch of her remarkable body.

He pressed a kiss to the space between her thighs. Laved her slick folds with his tongue as she shuddered in anticipation of each stroke. He lapped at the sensitive flesh surrounding the distended bundle of nerves, giving her pleasure while denying her the sensation she was so desperate for.

Until she begged for it.

Kayleigh applied the slightest pressure to the back of his head. "Parker, please. Don't tease me. I need you."

He grinned, his eyes meeting hers as he licked, then sucked on her slick bud.

Her head lolled back and she moaned with pleasure. She arched her back and her hips rocked forward. "Yes, yes. Right there. Just like that."

He increased his speed and intensified the pressure, bringing her to the brink. She was almost there and he was painfully hard when he halted his motion just enough to allow her to draw a breath. Then he drove his tongue inside her.

Kayleigh's body tensed and her eyes widened as she cried out with pleasure. Her heels dug into the mattress and her hips glided back and forth until she came hard, her muscles tensing and her core pulsing. His name on her lips.

He lay beside her, his lips brushing the shell of her ear when he spoke.

"I want to be the only man who gets to do that. The

only man who gets to hear you call his name in that breathless tone while you shatter to pieces."

Her eyes were watery as she pressed her palm to his cheek. "That's what I want, too."

Parker kissed her again, made love to her. As much as he'd enjoyed each of their previous encounters, there was something about this time that was so much more intense. Maybe it was because neither of them was trying to delude themselves into believing that this was anything other than love.

Kayleigh lay with her cheek pressed to Parker's chest as he slept, breathing softly. It was nearly two in the morning and they had an early flight, but she couldn't sleep.

As happy as she was that she and Parker were a bona fide couple now, she couldn't help worrying about how things would change between them once they returned to Magnolia Lake.

She'd been able to forgive Parker and let go of their painful past, but being part of Parker's life meant being a part of his family members' lives, too.

She'd managed to be civil to Duke Abbott during their business negotiations and during the party at his home. But she'd been tense and her stomach had been in knots the entire time. How could she spend casual Sunday afternoons across the dinner table from the man who'd capitalized on her father's impending death and her mother's illness to swindle her family out of their land?

She still wasn't ready to forgive Duke Abbott for what he'd done. Maybe she never would be. If she couldn't, she and Parker would be over before they'd even begun.

Twenty-One

Parker realized that they were both tired after their late night and early flight. Still, Kayleigh had been unusually quiet. Every time he'd asked if she was all right, she'd said she was. Then she'd gone back to mindlessly bouncing her knee as she stared out the airplane window.

Parker squeezed her hand. "Kayleigh, I'll make you a promise. I'll always be straight up with you, but you need to do the same. So if something is bothering you, I need to know. You can trust me."

She turned toward him and met his gaze. "These past few months together have been amazing. I want this—I really do. But being with you means I'll be spending a lot more time with your family. Which is great, except… I don't know if I can get past what your father did. I thought making him pay dearly for my building would satisfy the debt, but I honestly don't know if I can forgive him for taking advantage of my mother at the lowest point in her life. Especially when your family has so much."

"Thank you for being honest, sweetheart." Parker threaded their fingers together and squeezed her hand. "Kayleigh, I love you. I don't want anything to ever come between us again. There's only one way for you to resolve this thing with my dad. It's time you two talk and get everything out in the open."

"What could he possibly say that would make me feel better about what he did?" Kayleigh stared at their joined hands. "Other than camping, my best memories of my dad were those sober moments when we'd visit that old farm and he'd talk about all the things he wanted to do. He wanted to make it a working farm again. But my mother always dreamed of starting a little inn there."

"I know you don't think it'll help, but I need you to trust me. All I ask is that you give it a chance."

Kayleigh nodded and gave him a sad smile. "I promise to hear what he has to say."

Parker kissed Kayleigh's forehead and wrapped his arm around her. Now he would need to convince his father that it was time to tell Kayleigh the truth.

Parker had taken Kayleigh to her apartment to rest and settle in after they collected Cricket from Blake and Savannah's house. Then he went straight to his parents' home. After he hugged and kissed his mother and his sister Zora, who were working on dinner for later that afternoon, he found his father in the den. He was reading the newspaper with the TV on in the background.

"Hey, Dad." Parker sat on the opposite end of the

chocolate-brown leather sofa, where his father was seated. "Kayleigh is prepared to finalize the paperwork for the sale of her building. She can come to the office tomorrow morning."

"Well done, son." His father patted his knee. "I know it wasn't fair that the lion's share of the responsibility fell to you, but I'm thrilled we could do this for your mother."

"Me, too. Only it turned out that this was the best possible thing that could've ever happened to me, Dad. I'm in love with Kayleigh, and she loves me, too. We might never have gotten together if it wasn't for this project. So thank you for pushing me."

"You and Kayleigh are an item now?" The elder Abbott's expression indicated that he was genuinely happy for him, but his brows furrowed with a hint of concern. "I'm glad to hear it, son. Kayleigh is a wonderful young woman."

"She is, and I want her to feel the same way about you, Dad." Parker scooted to the edge of his seat. "But you know what she thinks of you."

"We can't control the things people believe about us, son. We can only make sure they aren't true." His father sipped from the large glass of sweet tea that left a condensation ring on the newspaper he'd been reading.

"Most of the time," Parker agreed. "But in this case, we both know that isn't true."

"What are you talking about, son?"

"I know everything, Dad. I've seen the original paperwork. After the incident with Savannah going through our archives, I started reviewing them a little at a time.

I wanted to make sure there weren't any other family secrets I should know about. That's when I discovered the truth. Now it's time that Kayleigh knows, too."

"Whatever you think you know, son, is best left in those archives." His father clicked the remote off, lines forming between his furrowed brows. "Things are the way they are for reasons you don't understand."

"Dad, whatever promises you made back then, I'm sure they were made for noble reasons. But circumstances change. I love her, Dad, but we both know there's no way that this relationship can work unless she learns the truth."

"Parker, you'll just have to find another way to convince her." His father walked over to the bar and refilled his glass.

"No, Duke, Parker is right. Kayleigh needs to hear the truth, and she needs to hear it from you. Please." His mother stepped inside the room and squeezed his arm.

"But I made a promise," his father insisted.

"That promise was made to protect Kayleigh, but it hasn't. It's isolated her and left her feeling resentful and alone. That isn't what her mother wanted for her. And it isn't what I want for Parker," his mother pleaded. "This secret will keep the two of them apart."

Duke sighed and nodded begrudgingly. "If you really think it's in the girl's best interest, I'll tell her."

Parker gave his mother a long hug. "Thanks, Mom." She smiled and kissed his cheek.

"Thanks, Dad." He gave his father a quick hug, then pulled out his phone to call Kayleigh. He didn't want to wait another minute to make things right between two of the people he loved most in the world.

* * *

Kayleigh clutched Parker's hand as he led her into his parents' home. He'd been adamant that she and Duke needed to talk right away. So she'd agreed to come to dinner and to listen to what his father had to say.

He led her inside the den, where his father was watching TV. Duke turned off the television, his shoulders tensing. "Have a seat, Kayleigh."

She shifted her gaze to Parker, who'd released her hand. "You won't be joining us?"

"I think you two should talk alone. But I'll be right down the hall in the kitchen if you need me. I promise." Parker gave her a quick, reassuring kiss.

It felt odd with Duke staring at them.

Parker left, closing the door behind him.

Kayleigh sank into a chair, her hands folded in her lap and her gaze not meeting Duke's. "Parker said that we should talk."

"Can I get you a glass of tea or lemonade? Maybe a bottle of water?"

"No, thank you. I'd really just like to hear what it is you have to say for yourself." Her voice wavered slightly.

"Fair enough." He nodded gravely. "Kayleigh, I don't know if your mother ever told you that I was sweet on her back in high school. But she was head over heels for your father."

"I know." It was one of the things her mother had reminded her father of whenever he was feeling sorry for himself or jealous of Duke and the Abbotts. *I chose you, not him.* "She said you two were good friends."

"We were." He smiled sadly.

"If that's true, Mr. Abbott, how could you have treated her so cruelly." Kayleigh maintained a respectful tone though she didn't mince words. Parker said he wanted her to have an honest conversation with his father. She'd taken him at his word.

Duke grimaced in response, as if her accusation had caused him physical pain.

Good. She'd drawn first blood.

"I realize this is an uncomfortable conversation for both of us, Kayleigh. And I know that you're angry because the money I paid your mother wasn't nearly the value of her property. But what you couldn't have known is that it was your mother who insisted I only give her a small percentage of the land's value."

"Why would she have done that? My father was dying and the medical bills had sucked up what little she and my father had managed to save for our college tuition." Kayleigh gripped the armrest of the chair. She'd promised to be civil, but she wouldn't stand for lies, not even from the high-and-mighty Duke Abbott.

"My father had offered to buy her father's land several years before. So she struck up a deal. She only wanted one quarter of the land's value in cash. The rest was used here." Duke handed Kayleigh a yellowing manila folder. "You'll find the answers to all of your questions in there."

Kayleigh reluctantly opened the folder. Her and her sister's names were all over college-scholarship paperwork. She recognized their signatures. "How'd you get my financial information?"

"It's typical that the organization granting a scholarship maintain a record of all documentation."

Kayleigh's eyes widened and she stared at Duke for a moment. She reviewed the documents again. Her heart pounded in her chest.

"Are you saying that King's Finest paid all of our college tuition and boarding through these scholarships?"

He slid back in his seat and crossed one leg over the other. "Initially the money came from the difference between the price I paid for the land and what it was actually worth, as well as interest. But your mother implored me to see to it that you girls were cared for throughout your college years. So when that initial infusion of cash ran out, yes, King's Finest kicked in. You and Evelisse were our first scholarship recipients, though you didn't know it. And you're the reason we've done a scholarship program ever since."

"I don't understand, Mr. Abbott." Tears stung her eyes and her voice broke. "Why didn't she just leave the money to Evvy and me?"

"Your mother was afraid that neither of you was ready for that kind of responsibility. That you'd squander the money within a year and be left with nothing."

Kayleigh wiped away tears. As much as she hated hearing that, she knew it was probably true. And, it seemed, her mother had played on Duke's affection for her, knowing he'd make up the difference once the money from the sale of the land ran out.

"So you've been our benefactor all this time? Why didn't you say something?" Kayleigh's chest ached and her stomach was tied in knots as she recalled all the awful things she'd thought and said about Duke Abbott.

"I made a promise to your mother that I wouldn't tell

you where the money came from. She knew how you felt about Parker and our family by association. She knew her baby girl well enough to know you'd never accept what you felt was a handout. So she asked me to handle it anonymously. I promised I would, so I kept my word." Duke sighed, leveling his gaze with hers. "Even though it was one of the hardest things I've ever had to do."

"Why are you finally telling me now?" Kayleigh asked through tears.

"Because my son loves you something fierce. And he and my wife believe your mother wouldn't have wanted me to continue keeping this secret when it's doing you more harm than good." Duke squeezed Kayleigh's arm. "I only hope, now that you know, that you feel my decision was justified."

Kayleigh nodded, eagerly, tears streaming down her face. They both stood and she hugged the man tightly. "I'm so sorry, Mr. Abbott. I can't thank you enough. I hope you can forgive me for mischaracterizing you the way I did."

"There's nothing to forgive. You didn't know the whole story. I would've felt the same way, too."

There was a tap at the door and Parker stuck his head inside. "Just checking on you two. Everything okay?"

Kayleigh nodded. She kissed Duke on his cheek, before he excused himself and left them alone in the room.

"Thank you, Parker. For everything." Kayleigh threw her arms around him and hugged him tightly. Then she lifted onto her toes and planted a soft kiss on his lips.

He wound his arms around her waist. "I love you, Kayleigh."

Her mouth stretched in a wide grin; her heart was so full of love for him. "I love you, too, Parker."

"Good." He nuzzled her neck. "Because I have a request."

"No, Parker, we are not going down to that workroom." She laughed, remembering when they'd kissed for the first time there.

He smirked. "Fine, then I have another question."

"Shoot."

"It's about that ring. I promised my friend I'd ship it back as soon as we returned."

"Aww." Kayleigh pouted as she held out her hand and studied the ring's intricacies. "It's so gorgeous. I'm going to miss it."

"Well, that's the thing. Since it's so well-suited to you, and since we're two misfit toys best suited for each other and we've finally nailed this whole fake-fiancé thing…maybe instead of returning the ring, we keep it. On the condition that you agree to graduate from being my fake fiancée to being my real one."

"Parker, did you just ask me to marry you?"

"Not very well, apparently." He grinned. "So let me try again."

Parker got on one knee and held her hand. "Kayleigh, I've never been happier than I have these past three months. You've made me see myself and the world in a different light. Every corny romantic comedy where the guy declares that the woman makes him want to be a better man… I get it now. Because you truly make me want to be my best self. Most importantly you've shown me how much better my life is with you in it. So Kayleigh Jemison, I am formally asking you to please be my wife."

Kayleigh nodded, tears streaming down her face as she pressed her lips to his.

Epilogue

Kayleigh had just finished up with a customer who'd commissioned custom jewelry sets for her bridesmaids when Parker came into the shop with Cricket on his heels.

"If it isn't my incredibly handsome fiancé." They'd been engaged for less than a month and it still made her giddy to call him that. "What brings you here in the middle of the day with Cricket in tow?"

Kayleigh stepped out from behind the counter. She petted Cricket and accepted a kiss from Parker.

"I brought you a little something." He grinned.

"Another offer?" she teased.

"Of sorts." He held out a large brown envelope.

Kayleigh raised a brow, accepting the envelope and opening it. The smile quickly faded from her face as she read the document.

"Is this a quitclaim deed for my family's land?" The type had gone blurry through her sudden tears.

"Not all of it, of course." She knew the Abbotts had developed some of the land, so that made sense. "But our family took a vote. We won't expand any farther on the land. We have plenty of additional property to work with, when the need arises."

"Why?" Her voice broke as tears wet her cheeks. "Why would your family do this?"

"Consider it an engagement present from my father."

"To us?"

"To you." He cradled her cheek. "It's yours, free and clear. Regardless of what happens between us. Your family's land, at least some of it, belongs to you again."

"This is a truly incredible gift… Thank you, Parker." Kayleigh swiped at the tears staining her heated cheeks.

In light of everything Duke had already done for her and Evvy, it didn't feel right for him to gift the land to her. Especially when they had generously paid her far more than her building was worth.

"As much as I appreciate the gift, and I truly do appreciate it, I don't expect charity from your family. I'd like to pay for the land. What does Duke think is fair?"

"This isn't charity, babe. You're family now." Parker pressed a quick kiss to her lips. "My dad wants to do this for you, and he's firm about this. He won't take a penny from you for it."

Kayleigh couldn't stop the tears from sliding down her cheek. She jumped into Parker's arms and gave him a big kiss. One that made her contemplate locking the door and turning the Closed sign so they could have an informal celebration.

"There's something I forgot to mention." He interrupted their kiss before she could float her idea of an afternoon romp in the storeroom.

"What is it?" She tried not to sound aggravated.

"The land is yours to do with as you please. So no pressure. But what we think would be really lovely there is a little inn. Maybe just five or ten rooms. We'd even be willing to invest in such a venture."

"That would've made my mom so happy." Fresh tears spilled down her cheeks. "It's a fantastic idea, babe. I love it. And I love you, Parker."

He cradled her to his chest, her head tucked beneath his chin. "Love you too, Kayleigh. Always have, always will."

* * * * *

If you loved Parker and Kayleigh's story,
find out who returns from Max's past to challenge
him in the boardroom and reclaim his heart,
as Reese Ryan's series The Bourbon Brothers
continues in November 2019.

Available wherever Harlequin Desire is sold.

COMING NEXT MONTH FROM

HARLEQUIN®
Desire

Available May 7, 2019

#2659 THAT NIGHT IN TEXAS
Texas Cattleman's Club: Houston • by Joss Wood
When an accident sends Vivian Donner to the hospital, Camden McNeal is shocked to find out he's her emergency contact—and the father of her child. As floodwaters rise, he brings his surprise family home, but will their desire last through a storm of secrets?

#2660 MARRIAGE AT ANY PRICE
The Masters of Texas • by Lauren Canan
Seth Masters needs a wife. Ally Kincaid wants her ranch back after his family's company took it from her. It's a paper marriage made in mutual distrust...and far too much sizzling attraction for it to end conveniently!

#2661 TEXAN FOR THE TAKING
Boone Brothers of Texas • by Charlene Sands
Drea McDonald is determined to honor her mother's memory even though it means working with Mason Boone, who was the first man to break her heart. But as old passions flare, can she resist the devil she knows?

#2662 TEMPTED BY SCANDAL
Dynasties: Secrets of the A-List • by Karen Booth
Matt Richmond is the perfect man for Nadia Gonzalez, except for one slight hitch—he's her boss! But when their passion is too strong to resist, it isn't long before a mysterious someone threatens to destroy everything she's worked for...

#2663 A CONTRACT SEDUCTION
Southern Secrets • by Janice Maynard
Jonathan Tarleton needs to marry Lisette to save his company. She's the only one he trusts. But in return, she wants one thing—a baby. With time running out, can their contract marriage survive their passion...and lead to an unexpected chance at love?

#2664 WANTED: BILLIONAIRE'S WIFE
by Susannah Erwin
When a major deal goes wrong, businessman Luke Dallas needs to hire a temporary wife. Danica Novak, an executive recruiter, agrees to play unconventional matchmaker—for the right price. But when no one measures up, is it because the perfect woman was at his side all along?

YOU CAN FIND MORE INFORMATION ON UPCOMING HARLEQUIN® TITLES, FREE EXCERPTS AND MORE AT WWW.HARLEQUIN.COM.

HDCNM0419

"You live in a secluded paradise." Rain started, a light sprinkling that grew stronger in seconds until it lashed the car windows. The interior immediately fogged—probably from her accelerated breathing.

Jack smiled. "There are other houses." The wipers added a rhythmic thrum to the sound of the rainfall. "The mature trees make it seem more remote than it is." Rather than take the driveway to the front of the house, he pulled around back to a carport. "The garage is filled with tools, so Brodie helped me put up a shelter as a temporary place to park."

Ronnie was too busy removing her seat belt and looking at the incredible surroundings to pay much attention to where he parked—until he turned off the engine. Then the intoxicating feel of his attention enveloped her.

Her gaze shot to his. *Think of your future*, she told herself. *Think of how he'll screw up the job if he sticks around.*

He'd half turned to face her, one forearm draped over the wheel. After his gaze traced every feature of her face with almost tactile concentration, he murmured, "We'll wait here just a minute to see if the storm blows over."

Here, in this small space? With only a console, their warm breath and hunger between them?

Did the man think she was made of stone?

She swallowed heavily, already tempted beyond measure. A boom of thunder resonated in her chest, and she barely noticed, not with her gaze locked on his and the tension ramping up with every heartbeat.

Suddenly she knew. No matter what happened with the job, regardless of how he might irk her, she'd never again experience sexual chemistry this strong and she'd be a fool not to explore it.

She'd like to think she wasn't a fool.

"Jack…" The word emerged as a barely there whisper, a question, an admission. Yearning.

As if he understood, he shifted toward her, his eyes gone darker with intent. "One kiss, Ronnie. I need that."

God, she needed it more. Anticipation sizzling, heart swelling, she met him halfway over the console.

His mouth grazed her cheek so very softly, leaving a trail of heat along her jaw, her chin. "You have incredible skin."

Skin? Who cared about her skin? "Kiss me."

"Yes, ma'am." As his lips finally met hers in a bold, firm press, his hand, so incredibly large, cupped the base of her skull and angled her for a perfect fit.

Ronnie was instantly lost.

She didn't recall reaching for him, but suddenly her fingers were buried in his hair and she somehow hung over the center console.

They were no longer poised between the seats, two mouths meeting in neutral ground. She pressed him back in his seat as she took the kiss she wanted, the kiss she needed.

Whether she opened her mouth to invite his tongue, or his tongue forged the way, she didn't know and honestly didn't care, not with the heady taste of him making her want more, more, *more*.

Don't miss Lori Foster's Slow Ride,
available soon from HQN Books!

Want to give in to temptation with
steamy tales of irresistible desire?

Check out **Harlequin® Presents®**,
Harlequin® Desire and
Harlequin® Kimani™ Romance books!

New books available every month!

CONNECT WITH US AT:

Facebook.com/groups/HarlequinConnection

 Facebook.com/HarlequinBooks

 Twitter.com/HarlequinBooks

 Instagram.com/HarlequinBooks

 Pinterest.com/HarlequinBooks

ReaderService.com

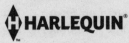

**ROMANCE WHEN
YOU NEED IT**

PGENRE2018